In The
Attic

Other Bella Books by Jackie Calhoun

Abby's Passion
Awakenings
Careful What You Wish For
The Education of Ellie
End of the Rope
Lifestyles
Life's Surprises
Looking for Julie
Obsession
Outside the Flock
Roommates
Seasons of the Heart
Serendipity
Triple Exposure
When We Were Young
Woman in the Mirror
Wrong Turns

About the Author

Jackie Calhoun is the author of twenty-eight novels. She lives with her partner in Northeast Wisconsin. You can find her on Facebook.

In The
Attic

Jackie Calhoun

BELLA
BOOKS
2022

Copyright © 2022 by Jackie Calhoun

Bella Books, Inc.
P.O. Box 10543
Tallahassee, FL 32302

All rights reserved. No part of this book may be reproduced or transmitted in any form or by any means, electronic or mechanical, including photocopying, without permission in writing from the publisher.

This is a work of fiction. Names, characters, businesses, places, events and incidents are either the products of the author's imagination or used in a fictitious manner. Any resemblance to actual persons, living or dead, or actual events is purely coincidental. The publisher does not have any control over and does not assume any responsibility for author or third-party websites or their content.

Printed in the United States of America on acid-free paper.

First Edition - 2022

Editor: M.E. Conway
Cover Designer: Heather Honeywell

ISBN: 978-1-64247-358-2

PUBLISHER'S NOTE

The scanning, uploading, and distribution of this book via the Internet or via any other means without the permission of the publisher is illegal and punishable by law. Please purchase only authorized print or electronic editions, and do not participate in or encourage electronic piracy of copyrighted materials. Your support of the author's rights is appreciated.

Acknowledgments

Thanks to Jessica and Linda and Bella's staff for their dedication and professionalism and for publishing my books over the years.

Dedication

To Diane

PART I

CHAPTER ONE

Evie awakened with a start and sat straight up in bed. Immobilized by fear, she listened to footsteps moving around downstairs. The clock on the nightstand read 12:32 a.m. She was alone in the house, without a weapon. Not that she knew how to use a gun. She'd probably shoot herself.

Her mind foraged for a safe place to hide. Under the bed? First place an intruder would look. Out the window onto the roof? It was raining, the drops sliding down the glass, and the roof would be slippery. In a closet? There were two closets— one with a huge traveling trunk and the other with a door on the end that opened into an attic space. She'd be trapped in either, but less so in the attic.

She slid out of bed and straightened the covers so that it looked like no one had been in it, then crept toward the closet just as she heard the first footfall on the stairs. With long, panicky steps, she slipped inside the closet and made her way around the suitcases and winter coats to the far end, where she fumbled for the door handle and pulled—gently at first and then with a hard jerk. Cold air rushed at her and she grabbed an old blanket from a stack on the floor and hurried inside, shutting the door quietly behind her.

The floors were old wood, and she picked her bare feet up carefully, not wanting splinters. Cobwebs—at least she hoped they weren't spiders' webs—brushed against her. She wished she had a flashlight because it was dark as sin, but a light would give her away if anyone opened the door.

She bumped into something solid and thought her heart had stopped until it picked up speed again. A scream came out as a squeak, as she adjusted to the lack of light. Shadows emerged where a few seconds before there had been only a black impenetrable curtain. The shadows turned into objects, mostly boxes, along with a few pieces of furniture covered with tattered, filthy sheets. She sat down on a chair that was behind a dresser. Dust rose around her as she wrapped herself in a blanket. She heard someone rooting around in the closet and held her breath.

A light bounced around the attic, missing her legs by inches. She pulled her feet onto the chair. A scream caught in her throat. The door shut. Paralyzed by fear, she remained motionless, although every nerve quivered, knowing he—it had to be a he—could be trying to fool her. Eventually, she fell asleep.

The door opened again. Footsteps echoed, breaking into her sleep. When the steps stopped, she looked up and saw a leering face.

She screamed and screamed.

A hand grasped her shoulder. "For Christ's sake, get a grip, Evie. What are you doing in here?"

The familiar voice penetrated her fear and her eyes popped open midway into another scream. "Ted, thank God you're home," she whispered in a hoarse voice. "Someone was in the house. I woke up and heard him downstairs."

His mouth twisted impatiently. "That was me."

"No. You would have called my name."

"And what time was it? Around twelve thirty? I poured myself a little brandy and sat down with the newspaper."

"And who was it that came into the closet with a flashlight and never said a word?"

"I was looking for you and saw nothing but dust."

"Oh. I thought you were coming home tomorrow. I was scared senseless."

"You are senseless. Come on. Let's get out of here." He pulled her to her feet and led her out of the attic. "You're filthy."

She was tired. So tired that her arms and legs had no strength. She leaned against him, but he held her away with a stiff arm.

She washed her face and feet, put on a clean pair of pajamas and climbed into bed with Ted. He was turned away from her. She could hear him breathing, feigning sleep. After twenty-three years of marriage, she knew the sound of his sleeping.

She turned her back and eventually fell into a dream-laden sleep, where she hid behind bushes, trees, buildings, screaming her head off and no one seemed to hear her. The footsteps were behind her—relentless in their pursuit, finally catching up. She sat up, fearful and confused.

"Stop that screaming. How is anyone supposed to sleep?" Ted spoke through clenched teeth.

"Sorry. Bad dream," she mumbled.

Morning came. A gray light gradually filled the windows. She watched it bloom into daylight. Ted was gone from the bed. She figured he had moved to the guest bedroom. Never once had he tried to allay her fears. It seemed as if he was always angry with her.

The cat jumped on the bed with a loud meow. He brushed her face with his whiskers and purred. Where had he been last night? Had it been real? He meowed in her ear. She laughed. "Okay, Georgie, time to eat." Knowing she'd never go back to sleep, she dragged herself out of bed, even though the clock read 5:55. Georgie would keep her awake, and besides, she didn't want to dream anymore.

She padded to the bathroom and after using the toilet, got dressed. She went downstairs with Georgie walking in front of her as if to lead the way. She had to gently push him on with her foot.

Ted sat at the table, drinking coffee and reading the Sunday newspaper. "Those fuckers just won't give him a break," he snarled.

"What fuckers won't give who a break?" she asked, pretending not to know as she fixed Georgie's breakfast. The cat rubbed against her legs and purred.

"Those goddamn left-wingers won't give the president any rope."

She put Georgie's food down. "So he can turn us into a Russian satellite?"

"I should have left you in the attic," he growled, looking at her over his glasses.

What had happened? He had once loved her. She would have sworn to it. "If something happens to me, you'll give Georgie to Angie, won't you?"

"What makes you think something is going to happen to you?" He cracked a smile and became handsome again. "You think I have a price on your head?" His laughter startled the cat, who crouched and stared at him.

"Promise me," she persisted.

He laughed harder. "You sure Angie wants him?"

She stood with hands on hips and mouth pursed.

"Why don't you give him to Rebecca?" he asked.

Rebecca was her best friend, whom she desperately wanted to talk to right now. Angie was her daughter, their daughter. They both loved Georgie, but Rebecca had a dog and Angie had roommates.

"Forget it." Chills raced up and down her body. It hadn't occurred to her that he'd go so far as to put a price on her head. Now she'd never feel safe.

"What's for dinner?" he asked, snapping the newspaper.

"You are so not funny. I could tell the police what you just said." She told herself she was crazy to aggravate him and added, "I thought I'd pick up a roasted chicken."

"We had one of those last week."

"Two weeks ago. I thought you liked it."

"Not every week."

"I can use the leftover chicken for soup." Which they'd also had two weeks ago. She poured herself a cup of coffee and took a gulp, burning her mouth. "Ted, would you be willing to see a marriage counselor with me?"

He looked up as if startled, before starting to laugh. "A little late for that, isn't it?"

"I don't know. Is it? And if it is, why is it?" She sipped the coffee and watched him.

"You're just clueless, aren't you?" He sounded disgusted.

"I guess I am. Want to tell me why?"

"You bore me," he said cruelly.

"Have you found someone who doesn't bore you? Is that the problem? If you want a divorce, why don't you say so?"

His eyes narrowed. "I suppose you think you deserve everything."

"Like what?"

"The house, the vehicles, the cottage, the investments I've made over the years."

Stunned, a picture of the cottage, its windows overlooking the lake, popped into her mind. She imagined the smell of pines, felt the warm sand beneath her toes. Longing built up inside her. She'd live in a hovel to keep the cottage. He seldom went there anyway.

"You planned well, didn't you? How much money do you think you can squeeze out of me?" he asked.

"I didn't plan anything. You're the one who seems to hate me."

He shoved Georgie away with his foot.

Georgie meowed indignantly and she jumped to his defense. "Don't take your anger out on him."

He shrugged and returned to reading the paper.

Fucker, she thought, picking up Georgie and snuggling him close. The cat pushed away from her and she set him down.

"I'm meeting Rebecca for lunch."

"Whatever," he said as if he were a kid.

Rebecca looked up from a booth in the Coffee Mill and took in Evie's frazzled appearance in one glance. That's what Evie loved most about her friend, how she could read her. "What happened?"

"He asked if I thought he'd put a price on my head," she whispered as she slid in opposite her friend. Then she told Rebecca the gist of their conversation.

Rebecca's green eyes widened as she listened. She reached across the tabletop and covered Evie's hands with her own. "You have to get out of there."

Evie looked at their hands and blinked back tears. "I can't afford to live alone."

A frown etched itself on her friend's face. Her auburn hair hung in perfect waves to her shoulders. With her eye-catching figure, Evie thought Rebecca was beautiful. She'd never understood what Rebecca saw in her. She felt sometimes she just dumped her problems on her friend. Rebecca could have anyone for a best friend, but she'd chosen Evie with whom to spend most of her free time.

"You could stay with us," Rebecca said. "John would understand, and Gracie loves you."

Evie smiled as she shook her head. "And I love her. But I wouldn't impose on you. Besides, I'd have to take Georgie with me. Duke wouldn't like that." Duke was Rebecca's dog, a chocolate lab that yearned to be a lap-sitter.

"Duke would be fine with Georgie. He would want to play."

Evie laughed. "Yeah. That's what I mean." She envisioned Duke chasing Georgie. It might be fun for Duke, but not for Georgie. She let out a sigh when their salads were placed in front of them.

Rebecca's hand again covered hers.

"It's okay." Evie thought of going home and chills raced through her.

"You could move in with Angie," Rebecca said.

"And the two other girls she lives with? I don't think so." She briefly thought of her son, Dave, who lived in a studio apartment. He was still a student at UW-Milwaukee.

She had started to feel unsafe when her kids left home. "Have you settled on a college for Gracie?" she asked.

"I think so," Rebecca said. "She loves UW-Madison, but it's hard to get into. She might have to go to UW-Eau Claire or La Crosse or Stevens Point first."

"Jimmy is at Madison. Does that help?"

"Just because he's her brother? I don't think so." She met Evie's eyes. "How did you manage when your kids left home?"

"I worried about empty nest syndrome before they left, but it was okay. There was less to do. You know? Less clutter, less clothes to wash, less cooking. And I got a job. No matter how Ted laughs at what I do, it fills the gap." She was a teacher's assistant for first grade, and she loved the kids and liked the teachers, some of whom might have been Angie's age.

Rebecca nodded at Evie's salad, which she hadn't touched. "Eat, Evie. You getting thin and skinny isn't pretty."

Evie grinned. "And I'm so pretty?"

Rebecca met her eyes, a forkful of food halfway to her mouth. "Oh, but you are. You look like a gypsy with that black, curly hair and those dark eyes and dusky skin. Or at least what I think of as a gypsy." The fork tines disappeared into her mouth, and she winked at Evie.

Evie grew hot. She'd forgotten how to handle compliments. Ted no longer gave her any. It was the wink, though, that made her blush.

Rebecca laughed.

Sooner or later she had to go to the store and decide what they were going to eat next week besides rotisserie chickens and fried rice. She also had to figure out what she was going to wear Monday.

"Call me, if you're afraid," Rebecca had said before they separated. She hugged Evie and gave her a little shake. "I mean it."

"I know you do. Say hi to Gracie and John."

Before the kids left home, she'd loved the weekends. Now it was the other way around. She didn't want to spend time with Ted, so she found things to do on the weekend—lunch out, walks in nearby parks, exercising at the Y, all with Rebecca. But then she began to worry about leaving Georgie alone with Ted.

When she walked into the kitchen from the garage, she put down the grocery bags and gathered Georgie in her arms, cooing at him. When she picked up his bowl to put food in it, she thought it looked kind of greasy, so she washed it in soap and hot water. Then she picked up his water bowl and imagined it smelled funny.

As she dumped the water and washed the bowl, Ted said, "What? Why are you washing his bowls?"

Her heart jumped at the sound of his voice. She hadn't heard him enter the room. "They were greasy."

"I gave him a piece of my breakfast bacon. He loves it."

"It's not good for him, and it's not good for you either."

"Jesus, Evie, you're the one who buys it." He headed into the den and turned on the TV.

She bought it for certain dishes she made, but she said nothing.

That evening, she watched *Doc Martin* with the cat asleep at her side, his legs straight up in the air. She planned to sleep in the guest room that night because she wanted to read. She didn't want to keep Ted awake like last night. That's what she told him anyway.

"Good. If you scream, I won't hear you." He came over and ruffled Georgie, who awoke with a squawk.

"Hey, don't be so rough."

"I was just saying good night."

"A gentle pat would suffice," she said.

"I'm driving to Chicago tomorrow morning. We're golfing with clients in the afternoon, and I have an early Monday meeting."

She looked at him after he gave her a peck on the cheek, instead of the mouth. He was tall with a full head of brown hair, turning gray. The dark bags under his eyes made them appear bruised, instead of dark blue. Yet he was well-built, probably because of all the golf he played.

Was he having an affair? She inwardly shrugged. Did she care? She would be insulted, of course. Was he beginning to feel old? Looking for a younger woman? As if anyone could bring back his youth.

"If I don't come home Monday, I'll call."

She turned back to *Doc Martin* and waved him away. "Good night."

CHAPTER TWO

When she awoke the next morning, Evie looked at the other side of the bed on her way to the bathroom. The sheet and comforter were thrown back. She thought she'd heard the garage door go up and down. So, he was gone already. Good. She had slept like the dead, ignoring Georgie's efforts to awaken her—whiskers in her face, meows in her ears, paws on her cheeks.

Only the cat's meows broke the silence, and then he too quieted as he ate. She turned on WPR's *Sunday Edition*, before making a pot of coffee and thinking about what she would do this day. It felt like a gift, yet she knew she should wash clothes, vacuum and get ready for school tomorrow.

The president was lying, this time about gangs of drug dealers trying to enter the country through Mexico. He was insisting that a border wall was the answer. Children of all ages had been taken from their parents. A judge had ordered they be returned to their families, but it appeared that the government had no idea from whom many of them had been taken.

What had happened to bringing the huddled masses yearning to be free? The president was making war against migrants fleeing murder and oppression.

After breakfast, she put on Georgie's halter and lead. The cat mewed loudly with excitement. He loved their walks, or at least, he loved going outside since he didn't do a whole lot of walking. He poked his head in bushes, flushing out rabbits without even seeing them run. He sharpened his nonexistent nails on trees, and he sat, staring. At what, Evie wasn't always sure. It could take a half hour to go two blocks. Sometimes, she picked him up and carried him home.

The young woman from next door was knocking on her door when she returned with Georgie. "Pam," she said with surprise. "Want to come in for coffee, and chat a bit?" She stopped short of the stoop and looked at her neighbor's angry face. "What?"

"Someone tried to kill Max," Pam said, thin-lipped and red-faced.

"Who? Why?" she asked, dread in her heart. Max was a large German shepherd that sometimes did his business in their yard. Ted became furious when the dog barked and barked, which he did when Pam left him alone. He was even more angered when he came upon Max's poop. Once he'd stepped in it and went on for days about doing something to keep the dog out of their yard. Evie had suggested a fence.

"Why should I pay for a fence? That woman with that damn dog should pay for it."

Shouldn't it be we, not I?

Now Pam said in a quavering voice, "Someone put poisoned meat in his dish. Fortunately, I got him to the vet in time." Sometimes Pam tied Max to a long lead in the backyard.

"What can I do?" Evie asked, appalled.

"Not long ago, your husband told me he was going to shoot Max if he didn't stop barking." And then her face crumpled, and she began to cry. "I can't stop his barking when I'm not home. Does he have to die for it?"

"No, of course not." She hadn't known this. She unlocked the side door, and setting down the cat, she urged Pam toward the kitchen. "I'll make fresh coffee." As if that would help, she thought.

"I don't want to be in Ted's house, drinking his coffee. He's a horrible man." A wrenching sob ended the crying, and Pam straightened.

"Yes, yes he is," Evie agreed, and the two women stared at each other—Evie alarmed by her admission and Pam looking startled to hear it.

Pam said, "Come over to my house. We can have coffee there."

Over steaming cups, Pam told her she was taking the dog to her mom and dad's farm. "He can bark his head off there," she said, her tear-reddened eyes locked on Evie's. "That's where I got him as a pup."

"I'm so sorry," Evie said, feeling guilty. The woman lived alone. Her dog was family. Besides, it was a terrible thing, poisoning an animal.

"I don't know if your husband did it. Other people have complained." She swallowed. "It's just that…" And she looked down, apparently unable to go on.

"I'll ask him."

"You think he'll tell you? It's a crime."

She thought of Georgie and trembled inside. "No. He won't tell me. I'm not sure he won't kill my cat." Admitting her fears for Georgie sounded dreadful. She raised her eyes to Pam's. She was awfully cute, Evie thought. It was the short wavy brown hair and the almond eyes.

Pam stared at her. "Why do you stay?" she finally asked.

Evie smiled politely. "Can't afford to go." What were her and Georgie's lives worth? "Besides, sometimes I think Ted is all talk, no action."

Pam laughed harshly. "Wish I believed that."

"I'm a teacher's assistant for first graders and I don't make much." She dropped her gaze, sure that Pam would laugh again. But it was why she couldn't move out.

"Really? That sounds like so much fun. I'd love to work with little kids instead of sick, old people." Pam got up and refilled their cups and put a few cookies on the table. "I'm a geriatric nurse. I thought I would see people who had lived full, exciting lives, but mostly I see the ill and infirm. It's hard to watch people die."

"People are living longer, but you probably wouldn't see the healthy seniors," Evie said. She saw them at the Y, taking yoga and spinning and Pilates classes. Her fingers disappeared into Max's scruff as she scratched his neck. The dog moaned and leaned against her.

"You keep doing that, you'll never get rid of him. Come on, Max." She lured the dog to her side and made him lie down.

Their conversation took off, till the dog began letting out little whimpers at the door. Evie looked at the clock, surprised to see that more than an hour had passed. Just as she started to say she had to go, although she didn't really, Pam leaned forward.

"I must take Max for a walk. My girlfriend is coming in half an hour."

"I was just going to say I should go."

"Yeah, your husband will be wondering where you are." Pam put a leash on the dog.

"He's out of town till Monday. Thanks for the coffee and cookie."

They went out the door, Max obediently sitting at Pam's side as she locked the door behind them.

"What a good dog he is!" Evie exclaimed.

"Except for the barking. I took him to dog obedience classes, but he can't seem to stop barking when I'm gone," Pam said as Max sniffed the ground.

"Are you and your friend doing anything interesting? A movie? Dinner out?"

Pam smiled wryly. "We've been together so long, we'll probably just watch the tube."

"It's wonderful to have a best friend, someone you can tell anything to." She was thinking of Rebecca.

"She's more than a best friend," Pam murmured.

Evie said, "Well, have fun."

She mulled over what Pam had said while she ate lunch. When she heard a car door slam in Pam's driveway, she got up and peeked out the tiny window in the door. Two women stood between the screen and door on Pam's small porch. They were kissing. She ducked as if caught spying and when she looked again, they were gone.

She spent the afternoon changing sheets, washing clothes, ironing for work, and vacuuming. She thought about Pam taking her dog to her parents' farm to keep him safe. And why. Somehow it made her feel complicit, being married to Ted meant she was responsible for his actions. And she envisioned the women kissing, which caused tingling in her groin. She remembered Pam muttering that they were more than friends.

She watched the news from the recliner while eating leftovers—fending off the purring cat with one arm and eating with the other. When one tiny piece of chicken remained on her plate, she gave it to Georgie. He was such a comfort.

She stayed up to watch the end of *Victoria* on *Masterpiece Theatre*, the one where Albert dies. Then she turned off the TV, and she and Georgie climbed the stairs. As she closed the blinds, she noticed the lights were off next door.

In the morning, she saw the car still in Pam's driveway. So, she was gay. So what? At least she wasn't alone. The car was a BMW. The woman had money, or she had spent all her money on a car.

Evie made coffee, took a quick shower and ate breakfast in between trips to the windows. She wanted to see Pam's girlfriend, but the last time she looked out the window, the car was gone.

At school, she greeted the teachers as if they were old friends and the children as if they were her own. The first graders clung to her as they told her about their weekends, and she listened as if what they had to say was enormously interesting. It was difficult getting them to settle in their seats.

She took the ones who were having trouble reading to another room and helped them sound out words. Listening to their young voices, often falling over words in a rush to tell her something, washed away her worries. To be with these children who were so young, so full of life, so enthusiastic, gave her great hope for what was to come. Sometimes a child was sulky or sad, making her wonder what was going on in that youngster's home. With encouraging words, she tried to make her time with the child positive. She often coaxed a smile from the boy or girl before returning him or her to the classroom.

Evie put her car in the garage next to Ted's. She'd been hoping he'd stay wherever he'd gone until Tuesday. She shut the garage door and went into the house, sweeping Georgie into her arms.

The television droned in the den. She set the cat down and fed him a treat. When she entered the den, she saw the back of Ted's head over the top of the recliner. Cartoons were on PBS. Why on earth would Ted watch cartoons?

She stared at the back of his head, reluctant to say anything. But then she called his name twice and got no answer. "Ted, are you waiting for the news to come on?" Certain that he'd fallen asleep, she walked quietly to the TV and turned it off.

Straightening, she looked at Ted. His eyes were open, which gave her a start. Then she saw the way his head was twisted to the side, how unnatural it looked, and his shirt had dark stuff on it. The newspaper had slid off his lap, his fingers still bent as if he was holding it. What she was seeing wasn't reaching her brain, not until she noticed he'd wet himself. Her hand flew to her mouth. On trembling legs, she made a wide berth around Ted.

Grabbing the receiver of the old wall phone in the kitchen, she dropped it twice before putting it to her ear and realizing there was no dial tone. Scared, her gaze roamed around the kitchen as she looked for her purse. It was in plain sight on the table. She pounced on it and fumbled inside for her phone. Her fingers closed around the cell's hard body and she punched 911.

Someone answered on the first ring. Evie whispered her name, forgot her address, then remembered it and told the lady something was wrong with her husband.

"I can't hear you, honey. Can you talk louder?"

She went outside and repeated her name and address and said again that something was wrong with her husband. "I just got home, and he's sitting in a chair with his eyes open and his neck twisted…and he wet himself." He'd be so ashamed, she thought.

She went inside and grabbed Georgie. She put him in the car and backed out of the garage and locked the doors.

When someone knocked on the car window, her heart banged in her chest. She'd expected to hear sirens and see EMTs, so she was surprised to see this man in regular clothes. He motioned for her to roll down the window. She did, just a bit.

"I'm Detective Jason Jalinsky, ma'am. You called 911?" The man held up a badge for her to see. His car was behind her and behind it was an ambulance with a man and a woman standing next to it. A police car was parked against the curb and two policemen were walking toward Jalinsky and her. Across the driveway, Pam stood outside, watching. Her hand was over her mouth.

Evie opened the car door and let them all into the house. She led them into the den and watched as an EMT lifted Ted's head, before lowering it gently. The woman felt for a pulse. She looked at her partner and shook her head.

The detective got on his phone and made a call.

Evie turned to stone. Isn't this what she'd hoped for at times this past year? That Ted would die? But she'd meant for him to die naturally, not like this—murdered in his own home, in his own chair. It made her hair stand on end. Who had killed him? And why? And was the killer still in the house?

"Mrs. Harrington, would you come into the kitchen with me, where we can talk away from all this," the detective said. "Sit down, please."

This is my kitchen, she thought, but she sat at the table across from him. Her mind was racing. She had to call her children and she wondered how she would tell them.

"Mrs. Harrington, where were you this afternoon?"

"What?"

He repeated the question, although it had registered retroactively.

She said, "I walked in and found him like that." She gestured toward the den. "Cartoons were on the TV. I turned it off and really looked at him. That's when I called 911." She dragged her hand through her hair. "Whoever killed him could still be in the house. The phone was dead." She pointed at the wall phone.

"My men will search the house," Jalinsky said. "Now, again, where were you this afternoon?"

Oh, so he's interrogating me, she thought. Should she ask for a lawyer? But she didn't know any lawyers. Besides, she hadn't done anything. She hadn't even been here.

"I was at school, where I work. And then I went to the store."

"What time did you get home?" he asked.

"Maybe a half hour before I called 911. I don't know what time it was. Wouldn't the woman at 911 know?"

"What school do you work at?"

"Heartland Elementary."

"And who saw you last?"

CHAPTER THREE

When they finally carried Ted out, his body in a sack, Jalinsky asked her if she had anywhere to stay the night.

"I'd have to take my cat." Only then did she remember Georgie was still in the car.

"Why don't you call a friend or relative and ask if you and the cat can stay overnight?"

"She has a very large dog."

"Well, maybe you can keep them in separate rooms," Jalinsky said patiently.

She crossed her arms. She was angry now, even though nothing could have persuaded her to spend the night in her own house.

"Call her. Okay?"

She turned her back and punched in Rebecca's number. It was late, too late to be calling anyone. The phone rang until the answer machine came on. Rebecca picked up when Evie spoke.

"What happened?" Rebecca asked.

Evie told her.

"Of course, you can come. Bring Georgie's things and he can sleep in the guest bedroom with you." Rebecca sounded horrified. "How awful, Evie. Why don't John and I come get you?"

"No. It won't take long." She didn't want Rebecca interrogated in the middle of the night. Fortunately, she had changed Georgie's litter on Sunday. Jalinsky carried Georgie's box and food and dishes out to her car. She brought towels in case Georgie puked. He hated riding in the car. So much stuff for one cat. After the driveway was cleared of vehicles, she drove away, only remembering to turn on her headlights when Jalinsky ran after her, shouting.

Rebecca opened the door, took one look at Evie, and said, "You poor thing."

Evie handed Georgie to Rebecca and went back to the car. She had quickly packed a small bag with her things. John was right behind her and began bringing in the other stuff.

After saying how sorry he was, John put everything in the guest bedroom and left Rebecca to talk to Evie. Evie slumped on the bed, Georgie jumped into her lap, and Rebecca put her arms around the two of them.

"What a great guy John is," she said, crying into Rebecca's nightshirt.

"I'm so sorry. Do you want to go to bed or do you want to talk?"

"Talk," she said, realizing only then how much she needed to talk.

She and Rebecca kicked off their shoes and lay on their backs, while Evie related the night's horrors. "Do you think I need a lawyer?" she asked when she finished.

"Yes. Yes, you do."

"Do you know any lawyers?"

"No, but I'll ask John tomorrow."

"I need to call my kids."

"You probably should."

"No point in calling tonight, though. The house is a crime scene."

"You can all stay here until they're done with the house."

Evie smiled grimly. She was suddenly so tired she felt sick. "Thanks, but maybe we can go back tomorrow."

She waited until seven a.m. to call her daughter.

"Mom!" Angie said with surprise. "Is everything all right?"

"Mmm. Well, no it isn't, sweetie. That's why I'm calling. Your father…"

"What's wrong with Dad?" Angie interrupted. "Did he leave?"

"What do you mean, Angie?"

"Did he move out? I know you weren't getting along."

"What makes you think that?" she asked, stunned. She'd always put on a good act for the kids.

"He told me."

"Oh. What did he tell you?" Evie asked. How could Ted have talked to their daughter about his relationship with his wife when he didn't even talk to her? She was furious.

"Just that you weren't getting along." Angie's voice sounded small. "What happened, Mom?"

"Well, I came home after going to the store after school and found your father sitting in his chair in the den, he'd been gone a couple of days…" she sputtered out.

"And? Was he all right?"

"He went to a conference and came home while I was gone." She paused and then forced herself to say the words. "He was dead. I'm so sorry, honey."

"Me too," Angie whispered. "How did he die?"

"I don't know yet."

Dave listened to his mother without interruption, then asked, "Who killed him, Mom?"

When she hung up, she looked at Rebecca and repeated what Angie had said. "Why would Ted tell Angie our marriage was in trouble?"

"Because he was a bastard."

Rebecca made a pot of coffee, which she and Evie were drinking when Angie and Dave came to the door. John had already left for work, and Gracie, looking as if she were in shock, had gone to school. Evie half-stood and then sank into her chair again. Her children looked so tired and disheveled that she began to cry. Sniffing, she forced herself to stop.

"Cup of coffee?" she asked.

Her two offspring said, "Sure," in unison. "Hi, Rebecca."

Duke galloped into the kitchen and gamboled around the newcomers, his big body bumping into them, the table, and the two women.

Both Angie and Dave ran their hands over his chocolate coat until Rebecca said, "That's enough, Duke. Down." And Duke dropped to the floor and rested his large head on a paw. "He loves company. When I go away for an hour, you'd think I'd been gone a year. He's so excited when I come home."

"That's a dog for you," Dave said. "Where's Georgie?"

"In the bedroom," Evie said.

They sat at Rebecca's kitchen table, mugs in hand, and looked at their mother. "Do you have any idea what happened?" Dave asked.

Evie said, "No. No idea at all."

"But where was the conference and who was he playing golf with?" Angie asked.

"I don't know. He never told me." It sounded odd even to her that she didn't know these things.

Rebecca said, "It's been a tough night for all of you. You're all damn tired, I'm sure, and everyone's nerves are on edge."

"But didn't you ask, Mom?" Angie asked, her voice high and angry as if she hadn't heard Rebecca.

"He never told me where he was going," Evie said. "I got tired of asking." Had she? Or had she not cared anymore?

"There's a cop car across the street," Dave said. "We drove past the house."

Her muscular son with the light brown hair and eyes. She and Ted had fought about him. Ted called him a fairy. She claimed he was sensitive. And he was. He'd make the salads for dinner, elaborate affairs with fruit and lettuce and vegetables. She'd thought perhaps he would be a chef. Ted had said he didn't need to go to college for that.

Angie said something. Evie came out of her reverie and looked expectantly at her daughter. "I'm sorry." Angie with brown wavy hair, petite and pretty. She'd always been more difficult than her brother, more critical of her mother. She burst into tears. "This is something that happens to other people."

"I know," Evie said sympathetically. She got up to comfort Angie, but Angie stood and ran to the bathroom off the kitchen and shut the door.

"I'm glad you're here for Mom, Rebecca," Dave said, pushing back his chair and hugging them both.

Angie came out of the bathroom a few minutes later and also hugged her mother and Rebecca. "Where is Dad?" she asked. "I want to see him."

"His body hasn't been released," Evie said. "I'll call Detective Jalinsky and see if we can go home." She dug around in her purse, searching for his card.

Jalinsky answered on the fourth ring. "Mrs. Harrington, can you come into the office?"

Evie hadn't expected this. She hesitated before saying, "If my attorney can come with me."

"Of course, but maybe we should make it tomorrow at one."

"I have two questions. Can my daughter see her father, and when can we return home?"

"The autopsy is scheduled for this afternoon, so it would be better to wait till tomorrow to see the body. We won't be releasing the remains until testing is completed. Please let us know the funeral home of your choice. And you may return home whenever you like. I will see you tomorrow."

"Who was the attorney John recommended?" Evie asked Rebecca, wondering what she was going to do for money.

"Charlotte Webster of Farley and Webster," Rebecca said.

"Why do you need a lawyer, Mom? It makes you look guilty," Angie said, looking as if she might burst into tears again.

"I told your mom to get an attorney," Rebecca said soothingly. "The police are looking for a suspect and sometimes they can't see past the spouse. The lawyer is someone from a very good firm."

"Can I see Dad?" Angie asked.

Evie explained why she couldn't see her father until the following day.

"Shouldn't we be planning his funeral?" her daughter persisted. Her pretty face had lost all color.

"I would opt for a graveside service with family and friends attending," Evie said gently.

"Why?" Angie challenged. "Why shouldn't we have a regular funeral?"

"Your dad didn't want one. We did talk about this. It's what he wanted, and under the circumstances, it seems the best way to go." She looked at Rebecca for support.

"Oh, everyone else can have a regular funeral, but not Dad. He was murdered."

Dave said, "Come on, Ang. Quit arguing."

"I'm arguing for Dad. God knows, you won't." Tears made their way down Angie's cheeks, drawing her features into a squint. She got up and said she was going out to the car. Dave sighed and followed her.

Evie let out a bigger sigh. She was very near to tears herself. "What would I do without you, Rebecca?"

Rebecca smiled wryly. "You're doing splendidly on your own." She gave Evie a hug. "Angie's tired and overwrought. Hang tight, Evie, and let the lawyer talk to the police. Wait a minute. I've got something for you." She went to the freezer and removed a casserole dish. "Take this with you."

When Evie fought back tears, Rebecca said firmly, "I always have one on hand, just in case. Call me tomorrow."

The knock on the side door window made her jump. Her heart beat in her throat as she went to the door and looked out. Pam stood in a glint of sunlight.

She stepped outside with Georgie in harness and on his leash.

"Is there anything I can do?" Pam asked, nodding at the police car. "Are they harassing you?"

"No. Just keeping an eye on me, I guess. They are only here for a couple of days." Jalinsky had asked if she wanted them to stay for two days. Maybe they were protecting her. Maybe she'd be next once they were gone. Chills coursed down her spine and lifted the hair on her arms. If there was a killer around, she should tell Pam. "Keep your doors locked."

"I always do." Pam's hand flew to her chest. "You mean I might be in danger?"

"We both might be."

"What did we do?"

"Witnesses." Evie lifted her eyebrows.

Pam eyes widened. "I didn't see anything. Did you?"

"No. I wasn't even here."

Pam said, "I just wanted to say I'm sorry, Evie."

"That yellow tape is a dead giveaway." She almost laughed and then sobered. "I didn't mean to make a joke." But she had to force down a giggle. What was the matter with her? First, she was scared, next she found the whole thing funny. Hysteria, she guessed. She focused on her neighbor's red eyes. "What's the matter, Pam?"

"Nothing."

"Is Max all right?"

As if in answer, she heard a deep, "WOOF!" They both smiled.

"They were here all night. The cops…"

"Did they keep you up?" Evie asked.

"Max kept me up, growling and barking. Look, I'm so sorry you had to go through this. It must've been awful."

"It was, but I spent the night at my best friend's house. That helped." They were standing in the driveway.

"I don't want to keep you from your walk," Pam said, glancing at Georgie.

"Why don't you come with Georgie and me?" Evie asked.

CHAPTER FOUR

Wednesday dawned early. She hadn't slept much the night before. She wasn't afraid because the kids slept down the hallway, and the police were parked across the street. This was their last night, though. But the bed had become an instrument of torture, so she was up before six and walking Georgie by seven.

It was a way to get out of the house. She thought she'd never be able to go into the den again. Maybe she should ask Dave to put the television in her bedroom; then she could have the cable company come out and attach it to the Internet.

Evie was halfway down the block when Georgie began to stare. She stopped and waited.

Dave bounded toward her, his long legs eating up the sidewalk. "Mom, where are you going?" His hair was wild as if he'd just gotten out of bed.

"Coming back from Georgie's walk."

"Maybe we should keep walking. I think Angie's finally sleeping. Neither of us slept much last night. Weren't you scared the killer would come back?"

"No. The police are out front, and you were down the hall, but I didn't sleep much either." Exhaustion flowed through her veins, yet she remained wide awake. Sleep would be a blessed reprieve.

"Mom, I think I'm going to major in the food service industry."

"Good. I think you'll do splendidly."

There was a pause before Dave asked, "Do you think Dad would be okay with that?"

"It doesn't matter what your dad thinks anymore. You don't have to try to please him." The cat had paused again to sharpen his clawless front toes on an oak. "Oh, come on, Georgie," she said impatiently. She picked him up and walked toward home.

"I never could please him, anyway," Dave muttered.

Neither could I, she thought. "He loved you, Dave," she said, hoping it was true.

"No, he didn't," Dave said. "He loved Angie. She did everything right. Boyfriends, prom queen, volleyball star. I didn't do sports."

"Janie was your girlfriend and you worked on the school newspaper." She'd defend him, even if he wouldn't.

He snorted. "Janie is my friend."

"It doesn't matter anymore, Dave. Let's go home and eat breakfast." She saw his hurt before he wiped it off his face. "You don't have to try to please him. You could have stood on your head and it wouldn't have mattered."

"Mom!" he protested.

"I saw how you tried and how he ignored your efforts."

Ted's disapproval had begun when Dave played house with his sister when they were little. It had accelerated when Dave had shown no interest in Little League. In high school, though, he'd helped manage the football team, making sure there was water to drink at practices and games, that school uniforms were cleaned, that there was a first aid kit on the field and the locker room was clean. He had complained about having to pick up jockstraps and socks.

Evie remembered him coming home exhausted and muttering to himself after practices and games. He'd quit doing it during his senior year. By then he was starring in high school plays and musicals. He had a wonderful tenor voice. Evie had tried to cajole Ted into coming to these events, but after going to one musical, Ted refused to go again.

He'd said, "He's a goddamn fairy, Evie. Makes me want to puke."

"He's your son and he's a terrific actor," she'd shot back.

"I'm ashamed of him."

Evie's heart hurt. "I'm ashamed of you." She didn't want Dave to be gay. It wasn't the easiest life. But he was her son and she loved him.

Ted sat down, put his head in his hands and moaned, "Why couldn't he play football or basketball instead of mincing around with a water bottle on the field or singing a stupid song on stage?"

She stared at him. "You bastard. Like you could do either of those things. I've seen your high school yearbook. You sat on the bench during games and you sure as hell weren't in any plays."

They hadn't spoken for a week until Angie had asked what was wrong. How easy it was for a kid to coerce her parents to at least give the appearance of getting along. However, she couldn't make Evie forgive Ted.

Inside her a fire had burned, slowly eating a hole in her stomach. It was only when Dave left for university that she let go of her anger. She recalled thinking then that now she and Ted could at least get along.

She met her attorney at two o'clock that afternoon. The offices of Farley and Webster were on the second floor at the downtown mall. Her kids wanted to come with her. Angie sat up front and stared out the passenger window.

"Mom, what are you going to do with Dad's car?" Dave asked.

"Nothing yet." Everything might be frozen, except her own account. She doubted she could afford this lawyer. She did have a checking/savings account of her own, but there was only $4,998.00 in it. She had checked that morning.

"I sure could use a car," Dave said.

"And mine is a beater," said Angie.

"I know," she said. They were fighting over the remains already.

"It's okay," Dave said, as if he had been reading her thoughts.

The reception area of Farley and Webster was quietly opulent. The lush carpeting and furniture exuded money. Evie might have turned around and walked out, except for the kids. Angie looked around and raised her eyebrows at her mother. Dave trod carefully beside Evie, who went to the polished receptionist's desk.

The young attractive woman had turned from her computer to greet them with a smile. "Mrs. Harrington?"

"Yes," Evie said.

"I'll tell Ms. Webster you're here."

Evie sat in one of the plush chairs and was reaching for a magazine when a woman called, "Mrs. Harrington?"

The woman walked toward her—tall, blondish hair, slate-blue eyes—dressed in a light gray suit with a blouse that matched the color of her eyes. Her hand was extended toward Evie. "Charlotte Webster."

Evie stood, reaching for the hand, searching the woman's face. She knew her from somewhere, maybe one of Ted's Chamber of Commerce dinners.

"Hi," Evie said. "These are my children, Angie and Dave. Can they come with me?"

"It might be better if they wait out here." The smile grew as the woman turned first to Angie and shook her hand and then Dave's. "Jaqueline will show you around." She smiled at the receptionist, who nodded.

Evie followed Ms. Webster down a short hall to an office that was both cozy and sumptuous. The carpet was a continuation of the plush beige one that had started at the elevator, the chairs comfortable, the desk polished cherry. The window looked onto the street that paralleled Main Street. The place conveyed subdued wealth.

The attorney shut the door and turned. "Evie, right?" she asked, a smile playing across her lips. She sat behind her desk. "I could hardly believe it was you."

A tall girl with a blond ponytail, running up and down the basketball court in high school, flashed through Evie's mind. "Charley! I thought I knew you from a Chamber of Commerce dinner."

"I avoid those like the plague." The smile disappeared. "I'm sorry about your husband."

"He turned into a son of a bitch," Evie said and clapped a hand over her mouth. "I shouldn't have said that, but I didn't kill him. I found him dead. The shock of my life."

"What happened that Monday?" Charley asked.

"I don't think I can afford you," she blurted, wishing it weren't true.

"We do pro bono work," Charley said, leaning on her forearms.

"It's just that I can't get into our joint accounts until everything is cleared up. I called the credit union. And I think Ted had other accounts. He didn't talk much about money anymore, and he was always going out of town but never telling me where." It was funny that she felt guilty talking about Ted this way, she thought, as if she was ratting on him. Maybe he was innocent of doing anything shady.

She struggled to tell Charley how he had treated her in the end. The things he had joked about, like hiring someone to kill her. Did she really believe he meant what he said? Charley probably had a husband who loved her and showed it. She was a knockout. "Your husband probably dotes on you."

Charley said, "Never met anyone I wanted to spend my life with. I guess I was too career-oriented. I worked as a public defender for years, but you can hardly live on that kind of money. So, I sold my soul to work here. I do most of the pro bono work."

"Well, I got myself pregnant by Ted," Evie confessed. "I took the easy way and married him. Maybe he never wanted to get married, but he worshipped our first born, Angie."

Charley was studying her. The intense blue-gray gaze flustered her. She shrugged. "I'm on leave, but I work with first graders as a teacher's assistant. Ted thought that was a piss-poor job. Not enough money, you know. Maybe when all this is done, I'll get certified and become a real teacher."

"If that's what you want to do, you should," Charley said. She sat up. "I'll have our private investigator look into your husband's activities. Let's see how much we can find out." She stood up and came around the desk. "I really am sorry you had to go through this, Evie."

Evie opened her mouth to say something about not spending too much money, but Charley said, "I'll keep the costs down. We have a good private investigator who will look into Mr. Harrington's affairs."

In the car, Angie peppered her with questions. "What did she say? What did you tell her? Did you badmouth Dad? Is that why you wouldn't let us go in with you?"

"I told her what I saw as the truth," Evie said. "I didn't want to upset you any more than you already are."

"And what was the truth?" Angie asked.

"What happened. How I wasn't home. How I found your father." There was no way Angie wasn't going to be hurt when she found out about her father's behavior. She might even blame it all on her mother.

"All right, Angie. Quit with the questions. It's stressful enough without making it worse," Dave said.

"No. It's okay," Evie said. "Both of you have a right to know what's happening. It's just that I don't know myself."

At home, Angie said, before heading to her room, that she was going back to work and if Dave wanted a ride to school, he better start packing. "We're leaving in the morning. Mom can call us when she finds out if there's going to be a funeral."

Relief flooded Evie. She didn't want to badmouth their father in front of either of them, especially not Angie.

Dave looked at his mother after his sister disappeared. "Are you going to be okay here on your own? You won't be scared or anything?"

She hadn't thought about being alone in the house at night. Of course, she'd be scared, but she couldn't tell him that. "You must go back to school sometime. I'll be okay." Maybe she could borrow Max.

The next morning, she hugged her children and waved goodbye in the driveway.

CHAPTER FIVE

She took a short shower in the locked bathroom. The shower scene from *Psycho* circled through her mind as she soaped and rinsed in record speed. She was pulling on a pair of shorts when she heard knocking…banging.

"Coming," she yelled, starting for the stairs, barefoot. When she opened the door, she saw Pam's back retreating into her house. "Pam!"

"Just wondering how you were doing." Pam jogged back to the door. "I thought you went somewhere with your daughter."

"They left. I thought you'd be at work."

"My shift doesn't start till seven p.m."

No wonder Max had death threats. She thought of Max barking at night and said, "Does he get along with cats?"

"He ignores them."

"Want to go for a walk with Max and Georgie? I've got an idea."

They were on their way around the block with the big German shepherd and the orange cat, but they weren't getting very far. Both Max and Georgie were smelling the same junipers, making Evie long for a gin and tonic.

"What's the idea?" Pam asked.

"Max can spend the night shift with me. He won't bark and he'll be good protection."

"He's one of those dogs that will lick you to death."

"But his bark and his size will keep anyone from breaking in."

"Okay. We can give it a try," Pam said. "I'll pick him up in the morning, but we better let him get used to your house."

Max sniffed around the kitchen, the den and living room. He came back into the kitchen and looked at Pam with puzzled eyes. Evie could almost see him worrying about being left behind.

"I'll bring him back before I go to work," Pam said before leaving.

Evie tried to coax Max upstairs when she went to bed. Georgie galloped up the steps, but Max stood at the bottom and watched them disappear. When Rebecca called around nine thirty, the dog was still whining.

"Sorry to call so late. Gracie's school had an open house. How are you?"

Evie told her the kids had left, and she'd had this brilliant idea of Max spending the night with her while Pam was at work. "I thought this was a win-win. He wouldn't bark and he'd be protection for me, but he's been whining since I went upstairs."

"Are the police still across the street?"

"They left late today."

"You and Georgie can stay with us," Rebecca said as she had before.

"We'll be all right," Evie said as she had before.

When she hung up, she opened her book and read as she did every night. Or tried to read. Max's whines had turned into yelps. Maybe she should make him come upstairs? But then she didn't know him that well. She called his name. No wonder Ted wanted to kill him, she thought.

She dropped her Kindle on the floor, put her reading glasses on the end table and slid under the sheet. She was drifting off when she felt something soft and warm against her leg. She jerked awake before realizing it was the cat.

Deep in the night, there was a banging on the door, accompanied by yelps. She dragged herself out of bed and crept downstairs. Pam stood outside in the whiteness of the light Evie turned on.

"I'm sorry, I'm sorry. Has he been crying the entire time I've been gone?" She had the dog's leash in hand. "I'll take him home. Maybe if he spends more time here during the day, he won't feel abandoned."

Evie went back to bed and stared at the ceiling for a long time before she fell asleep again. The ringing phone woke her in the morning. It was Dave, asking how she was.

She got up, wondering what day it was. She should call the school and ask to return to work. Later in the week, maybe she would do that. Now she would look for clues. There had to be a reason for someone to break in. But first, coffee.

She pulled out desk drawers and paged through old bills. Georgie followed her around for a while, lying down whenever she stopped to investigate something. Evie pawed through Ted's dresser drawers, shaking out his underwear and socks and sweaters and sweatshirts. In his clothes closet, she went through slacks and jeans and shoes. He had been very neat, and she put everything back the way she found it. She sat down on the bed, defeated, and the cat jumped into her lap.

Pam came over in the early afternoon with Max. By then, Evie was tired of looking. She had found a golf score wadded up in the recliner where he had died. She'd stuffed it in the pocket of her jeans.

They took Georgie and Max for a short walk. Black clouds hung as far as she could see. In the distance, thunder rumbled and streaks of lighting flashed. Rain began to spit as they hurried into Evie's kitchen, then a huge jolt of lighting flashed, followed by thunder. Max whimpered and Georgie bolted from the room.

"Guess Georgie doesn't like storms either," Pam said, unleashing Max, who crawled under the table once he was free.

"I like them at night, though. I guess they remind me of summers long ago." When her life was in front of her. Would she have married Ted again? "Decaf?"

"Sure." Pam pulled out a chair. "Not working?"

"Maybe next week, I'm thinking."

Saturday arrived and Evie hadn't found anything besides the crumpled golf score. Charley had invited her to lunch that day. She drove to Ridgeview Country Club, where Charley had left her name with the hostess. It was a private club. Outside, people were golfing, and in the distance, Lake Winnebago glittered in the sun. The hostess showed her to a table next to a window. Charley stood and shook her hand. Just like two men, Evie thought.

But Charley didn't look anything like a man. She wore low heels and her every move was graceful. Her hair fell to her shoulders where the ends flipped up, and her eyes smiled when they met Evie's.

"You know, you don't look any different than you did in high school."

"I didn't know you even noticed me in high school."

Charley arched an eyebrow. "Of course, I did. You were so smart in English. Made me want to disappear."

Momentarily speechless, Evie laughed. "And you were this gorgeous jock. Dashing up and down the basketball court when I couldn't even dribble and run without falling." Whoops. Had she really said gorgeous? But something was niggling her memory.

Now Charley laughed. "You had already read all the books assigned to us. And you hung out with Rebecca Hunter, always the top student in math."

"I still do, and she teaches math at Tech."

"How is she?"

"Sharp as ever." Charley had hung with the jocks. She and Rebecca had hung with each other. "Did you play sports at university?"

"I did. I got a scholarship to U of Iowa. Iowa's big on women's basketball. And you?"

"UW-Madison. To be honest, I was kind of lonesome at first. Rebecca had a scholarship to Marquette. I almost transferred to UW-Milwaukee, but I couldn't, because I had a scholarship too, albeit a small one."

The waitress was standing next to their table, setting down menus and water. They both ordered decaf and studied the lunch selections. When the waitress brought the coffee, they ordered. Soup and salad for Evie. An oriental chicken wrap for Charley.

She set the golf score tab she'd found on the table, smoothing it as best she could. "It was stuffed in the recliner where Ted died. It's all I could find. No receipts. No expense records. No phone, of course. But there's a logo and the name of a place on the top left-hand corner." She tapped the corner.

Charley studied it. "This is terrific, Evie. It gives us a place to start."

Encouraged, she said, "I'll keep looking."

"Can we meet again next Saturday?" Charley asked.

Evie looked for the bill. She asked.

"On the firm," Charley said.

That night Pam changed shifts and Max slept at home. Evie was still awake at nine thirty, when Rebecca called. She told her about her lunch with Charley.

"I never expected her to become an attorney," Rebecca said.

"Neither did I. She was a public defender before working for Farley and Webster." That niggling, elusive thought was making its way to the surface. "Do you remember what the kids used to call her?"

"You mean jock?"

"No, I mean gay." She was ashamed to call Charley names behind her back. But it wasn't something to be ashamed of. Her own son was gay.

"Yeah, and maybe she is, but who cares anymore?"

"A lot of people, unfortunately," Evie said, remembering Ted.

"She was a great jock, though. Everybody wanted to be on her team in high school."

"I remember. I was hopeless when it came to sports. You were much better." She remembered how she'd had to steel herself against ducking when a volleyball or basketball came her way. She thought the Phys Ed teacher took pity on her when she gave her a C.

"Nah, I wasn't any better. There are women's pro basketball teams, but you never see them on TV."

"I know. Women always get the shaft, don't they? Don't we?"

She panicked. She'd made her one call and Charley couldn't take her case. For a moment, she stood in the busy hallway, unable to make herself go back to that cell with the four sad women.

"Outta the way," the man behind her said, shouldering his way to the phone.

The stocky woman guard who had led her to the phones, grabbed her arm and marched her back to the dank cell. When the guard pushed her inside and slammed the door, one of the women threw herself on the bars, yelling, "Missy, Missy. I have to go home."

What woke her she didn't know. Maybe it was the clanging door. But there was no such noise here. The dream faded away and she felt around for Georgie. He was gone from the bed. Listening for him, she thought she heard someone moving around downstairs. She got up quietly, her heart banging against her chest, so hard that she could barely breathe. She made the bed and crept to the attic. This time the door opened without a sound. She grabbed an old blanket and disappeared into the darkness. She'd put on slippers, which she now kept beside the bed. They were as silent as bare feet. Webs clung to her as she walked with her hands in front of her. Still, she bumped into old furniture. Wrapped up in the blanket, she sat in the same chair as last time and pulled her feet up.

It seemed like forever before the door opened. She sucked in her breath, her body taut, her heart beating so loud she thought it would give her away. Georgie was dropped into the attic. He always meowed when he landed from any height. Evie's muscles tightened painfully. Her left thigh was cramping. She figured whoever it was guessed the cat would find her. Her ears strained for sound. She heard the door shut, but stayed in the same position, waiting for it to open again. When it did, Georgie jumped onto her lap, and she let out a little shriek.

Then something smashed her on the head and everything went black.

Georgie's paws gently patted her face. She opened her eyes to excruciating pain, saw the shadow of the cat and became so dizzy she squeezed them shut again. She puked, the vomit dribbling out the side of her mouth onto the floor, where she'd fallen. Everything went black again.

When she next opened her eyes, a purring Georgie was tucked next to her. A splitting headache nauseated her. She moved only her eyes. A meager light shone through the filthy window. So, it was morning. Maybe the man had left. She lifted her head and was overcome by dizziness. She squeezed her eyes shut and tried to sit up. Panting, she leaned back against her hands, eyes closed tight.

Georgie meowed loudly. He was hungry. She pulled herself toward where she thought the door was. She moved erratically, stopping to breathe and wait for the dizziness to let up. When she felt the door behind her, she turned slowly and walked her hands up it till she was standing. She grabbed the knob and leaned backward, but either she hadn't the strength or it was wedged shut somehow. When she could stand no more, she turned her back to the door and slid to the floor.

Georgie meowed in her face, and she pulled him close. "Shhh," she whispered. Head throbbing, she closed her eyes and slept.

Awakened again, this time by something pushing against her, shoving her across the floor. The door opening, she realized. Georgie was making a ruckus. Of course, he thought he was going to get fed. Instead, they'd probably both be killed, but she didn't have the energy to move, much less run. Anyway, there was nowhere to run.

"Evie, Evie." Someone was saying her name. It sounded like Pam, but Pam was at work.

"Don't move her. We'll call an ambulance," Pam said.

"Georgie. Hungry," Evie whispered.

"Wait. She said something." Pam was kneeling next to her. "What, Evie?"

"Georgie. Three ounces canned food in the fridge. And water. Pam?" Talking exhausted her.

"I'll feed him. What else?" Pam bent to hear.

"Call my friend Rebecca and Charley Webster of Farley and Webster."

"Okay. The EMTs are here to take you to the hospital. Which one?"

"AMC."

She felt herself being lifted off the floor and taken down the steps, swinging from side to side. Dizzy again. An EMT stuck a needle in her hand and she knew it was for a drip. Another needle. The pain vanished and so did she.

CHAPTER SIX

Voices nearby. Rebecca. Charley. Pam. She was still alive?

Another familiar voice asked, "Can you wait outside the room, ladies? I need to ask Evie a few questions."

The detective. What was his name? She couldn't remember.

"I will stay. I'm her attorney and she's not conscious."

She was, though. She was listening, afraid to open her eyes lest the dizziness return.

"We're trying to protect her." The detective sounded annoyed.

"Well, Detective, you're not doing a good job. She has a concussion. She can't be riled up."

"I know, Counselor. I'll be gentle."

"I never saw who it was," Evie whispered.

Charley and Jalinsky bent over the bed. "What?" Jalinsky asked.

"I never saw the person. It was dark. He came up behind me. I don't even know if it was a he or she."

"Okay. Charley, can I talk to you?"

Rebecca leaned over the bed and gently pushed Evie's hair back from her face. "Evie?"

"Georgie?"

"Pam took him home with her."

"Poor Ted." She had only felt anger, till now.

"What about Ted?" Rebecca sounded incredulous.

"Knowing he was going to be killed."

"You know that?"

"Just a hunch. This guy was looking for something."

"Did you find something?" Rebecca looked frightened.

"Just a score tab. I gave it to Charley."

"Good," Rebecca said softly. "I was so worried. You were supposed to call me Sunday."

Evie murmured, "Don't tell kids."

"I did tell them, but I also told them not to come home. You're coming home with me."

"What day is this?"

"Monday."

"I lost a day?"

"Now you know why we were so worried. Pam called the police, who broke into the house."

Evie was out of the hospital, at home with the cat and Charley, who was sleeping in Dave's room. She had stubbornly wanted to return home. Going somewhere else meant living out of a suitcase.

At first it had felt odd, having Charley in the house. But she was grateful. So much better than Max, whining at the kitchen door. Of course, he'd mostly gotten over that and instead waited patiently by the door for Pam's return.

Evie and Charley were playing cards and drinking wine at the kitchen table, the windows darkened by night.

"You shouldn't be drinking," Charley said.

Evie glanced at her. She was so beautiful. Shoving that thought out of her mind, she got up, grabbed the wine glasses and filled them with water. "My fault. Weekends are for wine." She sat down again.

"Hey," Charley protested. "I can drink."

"That's okay. We play better sober." And she proceeded to whip Charley at cribbage. "Lucky," she proclaimed, shuffling the cards. "I'm going to bed. Maybe with you here I can finally sleep. What are you going to do?"

"Stay up a while and read. It's only nine."

Evie stood, smiling at her guest. "You know where everything is. Right?"

"I do," said Charley. "Sleep tight."

Evie fell asleep with Georgie lying on top of her. Maybe the cat was afraid, too, was her last thought. When she woke up, it was morning, the window filled with light. Birds singing. She felt so fortunate to be alive.

She got up, dressed and went downstairs with Georgie. He purred and rubbed against her as she readied his food. She had the coffee going before Charley appeared in the kitchen, her hair still wet from the shower, dressed in a suit and low heels. Evie was scrambling four eggs with red peppers and onions in them. She put the toast down. "You look terrific."

"Thanks. You don't look so bad yourself. Can I help?"

Evie laughed. "Yeah, sure." She wore jeans and a sweatshirt. "You can put down the toast."

"It's that silky black hair."

Evie turned red. Charley calmly met her gaze, brows raised. They sat down to eat. This is nice, Evie thought.

"What are you going to do today?" Charley asked.

"Take Georgie for a walk. Look for clues. Fix dinner. Will you be here for dinner?"

"I wouldn't miss it. After five. I'll call you if something comes up."

She was left to clean up before Georgie's walk, but she didn't mind. What she did when she returned from Georgie's walk, though, was lie down and fall fast asleep. Then someone was shaking her arm, and her lids were glued shut. Was it after five already?

"All right. All right. I'm awake." She gazed blearily at a strange man with a knitted mask, covering his hair and face, leaving only his eyes and nose and mouth exposed. Her pulse jumped-started her. It was he. Even when strangled with fear, her grammar was correct, she thought, swallowing a hysterical laugh.

She sat up, leaning against her arms. "What do you want?" she whispered.

He roughly pulled her out of bed. "Tell me where it is." His voice sounded weird—distorted, as if he had something in his mouth.

"Where what is?" She looked down at her shaking legs. She didn't want him to think she could recognize him. Then he'd have to kill her.

"Your husband was a piece of shit. He stole from me."

"He was a piece of shit, but he never told me anything." She could hardly stand. Bravery eluded her.

He dragged her around the house, stopping in each room, asking, "Is it here?"

"Is what here?" she asked every time.

When they were back in the kitchen and she figured this was it, she braced her body against the wall. "Don't kill the cat. Please?"

"You don't know, do you?" he said, more of a statement than a question.

She shook her head. "He didn't talk to me anymore about what he did with his money, if that's what you mean." She hoped he noticed she was still looking down. It was hard to do, not to look out the window for the last time. Or look at the rooms. Kind of silly because she wouldn't remember anything once she was dead.

He let out a big sigh and said, "Turn around."

So, he was going to shoot her in the back. Or maybe he was going to choke her or slit her throat. Her legs began shaking again and her heart went crazy. Maybe she'd have a heart attack and die before he did her in.

She felt the bandanna cover her mouth. It was tied so tight that she had to concentrate on breathing. He jerked her arms behind her and tied them with the clothesline rope that was in the closet with the broom and dustpan. Then he tied her ankles together with what was left of the clothesline.

She heard the kitchen door open and shut and knew he was gone. She was alive. Why was she crying? Sobbing. Her nose running. She stopped, though, because she couldn't breathe. Patience, she told herself. She'd have to wait till Charley came back or Pam stopped by. Or the police checked on her. She was so uncomfortable. Lying down was worse and once down, she couldn't get up.

Georgie squatted next to her head and licked the tears dripping from her eyes.

What the hell was the matter with her? She'd just escaped death. She should be rejoicing. Her right calf began to cramp. She rolled around the floor, chewing on the bandanna, until she hit the table and everything went flying, including a serrated knife.

She awkwardly grabbed it, dropped it, grabbed it again, turned it around, dropped it, picked it up and began sawing at the rope that tied her legs to her wrists. She sawed till her hands cramped, forcing her to drop the knife. Her leg burned and she jerked her feet till the cramp in her calf eased a little.

The wall clock told her it was half past noon, and the phone rang again. It had started ringing around eleven thirty. When it had stopped, Rebecca asked, "Are you all right, Evie?" And then her cell rang and rang.

She had tried to scream but ended up with a mouthful of cloth. Of course, she knew Rebecca couldn't hear her. She had cried then, only stopping when her leg started cramping again.

This time Rebecca said, "Evie, call me when you get home. Okay?"

She tried to relax so the cramping would stop. The hours crept by. When she finally fell asleep, after another bout of trying to saw the rope in two, Georgie woke her up. Only fifteen minutes had passed. By the time she cut the rope between her tied wrists and ankles, it was nearly three o'clock.

She tried to stand, but she couldn't balance. Not even able to steady herself on her knees, she fell over. Frustrated, she kicked at anything and everything. Panting, she made her way to the far wall and pushed herself to a sitting position, stretching her legs before her. The cramping had stopped anyway. Now her shoulders ached and her wrists were numb.

Rebecca's face appeared in the kitchen door window, surprising Evie who tried to yell. The key turned in the lock. Of course, Rebecca had a key.

Running across the room, Rebecca cut her wrists and ankles free and rocked her in her arms. "What happened?" she asked, untying the bandanna and wiping Evie's face free of snot and tears. "How long have you been like this?"

"Since this morning. I thought he was going to kill me," she croaked. "He keeps getting in the house."

Rebecca helped her to her feet and led her to a chair. "I'm going to call Jalinsky."

Jalinsky called a locksmith, who installed extra deadbolts on all the outer doors before Charley appeared. By then Pam was also there. But Evie wondered how anyone could save her because she was sure the man would find another way into the house.

"What did he look like—eyes, hair, build, clothes?" Jalinsky asked. He was standing near Charley and was no taller than she was. But his neck was thick and his biceps strained against his shirt.

"I didn't look at him. I was afraid he'd kill me if I could identify him. Anyway, he was wearing a face mask."

Jalinsky said, "Good thinking."

Charley shot him a look.

Rebecca poured a glass of chardonnay and put it into Evie's shaking hand. Evie gulped it down. "Pour everyone one," Evie said, hand and voice shaking.

Jalinsky and the two policemen he brought with him waved off the wine, so Rebecca made coffee for them instead.

The others sat at the table after putting the room back in order. Evie had kicked over chairs and shoved the table askew during her struggles to free herself. They twirled the stems of their glasses and shot discreet looks at Evie, who was slowly downing glasses of wine.

Finally, Rebecca took Evie's glass away. "Drinking won't help. Instead, you'll feel worse tomorrow."

Evie put her head in her hands to hide the tears that came in tides. "I should have looked at him. Maybe they could find him then."

Charley studied Evie. "He had a face mask on, you said."

"He did, but I don't know what he was wearing or how tall he was or if he was skinny or fat or the color of his eyes."

"Certainly, you can forgive yourself for wanting to live," Rebecca said. She caressed Evie's arm.

She looked up, the whites of her eyes red. "I'm afraid to go to sleep."

Max had been sitting by her side. He pushed at Evie's hand, which had fallen to her side. Absently, she put her hand on his head and then looked at him in surprise. He'd never done anything like that before.

Evie smiled at Pam. "Is he comforting me?" she asked, amazed by this.

Pam nodded. "He knows you're upset."

Evie hugged the dog, who whined and licked her arm. "You sweetie, you," she said, croaking a laugh. "Who would have guessed?"

"He can stay with you during the day when Charley leaves."

"Oh, but that would be wonderful," Evie said. "Except Charley is going to get pretty tired of staying here."

"I'm not staying here tonight," Charley said, looking steadily into her eyes. "Evie and Georgie are coming home with me."

CHAPTER SEVEN

Evie was so tired when she arrived at Charley's condo, she hardly registered her surroundings. After giving Georgie food and water and setting up his clean litter box, she asked where she should sleep and was it okay if Georgie slept with her, because he usually did.

"Sure," Charley said, "but I think we should eat. You must be hungry. I am and I like eating with someone." She looked at the cat, eating as if starved. "And Georgie doesn't count."

"Oh, okay." Evie ran her fingers through her hair. She felt as if some important part of her was missing and attributed it to the wine.

Charley removed some Tupperware bowls from the fridge and made a couple of salads. "Sit down. Dinner will be ready in five minutes."

Evie ate without tasting but said everything was delicious. She helped clear the table, and Charley told her it was all right for her to go to bed. "Come on. I'll fill the dishwasher as soon as I show you your bedroom."

Evie's bedroom had a queen-size bed, a bookcase filled with books, and a private bath. "Does someone else live here too?"

"No, why?"

"You said you didn't like to eat alone, but if you live alone…"

Charley laughed. "I eat out most of the time, but usually with someone."

"Thanks, Charley, for everything," she said, suddenly dizzy.

Charley said, "I love company," and went off toward the kitchen.

Evie washed her face and hands, grabbed a book out of the bookcase and climbed into bed. She buried herself under the duvet that covered the blanket and sheet, dropped the book and fell asleep.

A three-quarter moon poured light through the window and across the beige carpeting. She had woken as she did every night, hearing something or someone. She sat up to listen better and realized that Georgie was not with her, even though she'd left the door open. Had the man found where she was and somehow broken in? Charley had shown her the deadbolts on the doors and locks on the windows.

Again, the noise, halting, like someone trying to find their way in the dark. There was no attic here. She had looked before getting into bed. The clock read 2:05. Heart hammering, she slid out of bed and crept to the door. No one in the hallway. She knew Charley's bedroom was next to hers. There was no use looking for Georgie. He would hide if someone scared him.

Opening the door enough to slip though, she locked it behind her. She crept to the bed where Charley slept and slid between the sheets.

Georgie was pawing her, trying to wake her so she could feed him. She curled up tighter and tried to ignore him. As if out of a fog, she remembered the door was closed and locked. He couldn't get in. She sat up and screamed.

"Hey, it's me—Charley."

Evie opened her eyes. She was shaking. "I heard him. The killer."

"Why didn't you wake me up?"

"I don't know. I thought maybe you would send me back to the other room."

Evie shivered under the blanket. When she heard Georgie meowing indignantly she put out her arms and pulled him close until he disappeared under the covers, his tail swishing in her face before he pressed against her body.

"There is no one in the house," Charley said, slipping into the other side. "You're perfectly safe."

But Evie heard her as if from a distance. She was almost asleep when she remembered the bedroom door. "Is it shut and locked? The door?"

"Wha…?" Charley asked.

It wasn't, Evie saw. She jumped out of bed and closed and locked it.

"What the hell," Charley said.

And then they were both quiet.

Charley and Georgie were gone from the room when Evie woke up. It was the most comfortable mattress she'd ever slept on, and the cover was light as down and just as warm. She hated to get up, but it was after nine. She looked around the room: the bed with two end tables with lamps, two dressers, one with a small TV facing the bed, a comfortable chair with a side table and lamp next to it stood by one of the windows. And a bathroom. The walls were painted off-white with different-colored rugs covering the wood floor.

She trotted down the hall to the guest room and used that bathroom. After walking around the condo, making sure just she and Georgie were there, she took a shower. Apparently, Charley had fed the cat. He would have been all over her by six a.m. had he not eaten.

She gawked at the kitchen. It was a chef's kitchen, and she wondered if Charley was a great cook. It was then she saw the note beside the coffee maker. She read it as she poured herself a cup and put it in the microwave to heat.

I fed Georgie. Coffee's made. If you want more, coffee in cupboard. Fix yourself some breakfast. I'll be home at lunch. We'll talk then. C

Evie wondered what they would talk about. Charley would probably want her to leave after all the disruption last night. She would go, but she trembled at the thought of going home. She could pay rent to stay, as long as it wasn't a huge amount. She still didn't have access to Ted's money, and if his money was ill-gotten, she wouldn't get any of it. She couldn't live on what she was paid by the school.

She looked at the food on the table—bread, butter, jam, granola. A bowl was there as well as the newspaper. She got milk out of the fridge, sat down and poured cereal into the bowl. While reading an article in the paper about Ted's murder, she heard a door open.

Instantly, Evie was on her feet, ready to flee. Then she heard Charley talking to Georgie. "Never thought I'd have a cat in my bed."

Charley walked into the room. "I didn't mean to startle you." She wore a beige suit with a white blouse and beige kitten heels. Her hair glowed in the light coming in the windows. It was sometimes hard to link this elegant woman with the one who played basketball in high school.

"Sit down and finish your cereal, Evie. I just came home to see how you are."

Evie sat, but she found it difficult to eat in front of Charley. "This article is about Ted," she said, shaking the newspaper.

"Is it? I didn't have time to look at the paper. Evie, I think you should stay here until they catch the guy who broke into your house. You're not safe there and I have plenty of room." She looked tired.

"I'm sorry I kept you up last night. I wake in the night and I hear him. Did you hear him last night?"

"That will probably take some time to go away. You can sleep with me till it does. Now I have to go back to work. I'll see you around five?"

"Do you miss basketball?"

Charley took a step back, her expression surprised. The question had come out of nowhere. "I do. I miss my teammates. College was even better than high school." She sighed. "Got to go."

And then she was gone.

Evie put the food away and explored the rest of the condo. It was large and circled from one room to another, except for the bedrooms, which were off a hall that led to the kitchen. There was a dining room with a table and padded chairs for eight and a buffet. Portraits of what might have been Charley's family hung from the walls. A living room with a leather couch and three chairs, end tables with lamps beside each. On the walls were pictures of a sailboat bending to the wind in high waters, a few houses nestled in the mountains, a rundown farm with an ancient tractor in front of a sagging barn, and on the end wall between two tall windows, a massive electric fireplace. The front door was situated in the living room.

In the den were two recliners and a love seat, which looked toward a huge TV. Here there were no pictures on the walls. Between the kitchen and den was a half bath. She opened a door to a two-and-a-half car garage that was empty. And then there were three bedrooms, each with a full bathroom. The furnishings were expensive. Except for the bedrooms, the place made her think it was furnished for show or just to fill space.

Why would someone who lived alone buy such a large place? It was a question she couldn't ask and only ponder. Charley might not always have been alone. Perhaps someone else had lived here too, at another time.

She picked up the book she'd chosen last night, *One Plus One* by JoJo Moyes and read at the kitchen table. When someone rang the doorbell, she jumped. Should she answer? Maybe Charley forgot her key. She walked through the dining and living rooms with trepidation. It could be the killer. He might have followed her here. She peeked through the peephole, saw Rebecca and laughed.

"Hi, girlfriend," she said, swinging the heavy door open. "Come on in."

"I haven't much time. Just thought I'd swing by and see how you were doing."

"Time enough for a cup of coffee?"

"A quick one. Are you alone?"

"Yep."

They briefly paused in the living room. "Wow. Impressive. It doesn't look like she spends much time in here, though."

"The TV is in the den. It's a lot like this. Unused."

When they got to the kitchen, Rebecca sucked in her breath. "This looks like those cooking show kitchens."

"Doesn't it?" She put two cups of coffee in the microwave.

"Why are you reading in here?" Rebecca picked up the book. "I read this. Her books are good."

"This one is. Sit down. I feel comfortable here."

"I drove past your house today. That detective was there, knocking on the door. Maybe you should call him."

"I don't want to talk to him. I told him all there was to tell." Evie felt like she was deflating. "I can't help. I didn't look at him hard enough."

"His shoes?" Rebecca asked.

A picture appeared in Evie's mind. Tennis shoes. Old ones whose brand and color were too faded to tell. Ratty laces and no socks. "The man was poor." She felt a moment of excitement, which was soon mixed with fear. Next time maybe he would kill her. She shivered.

"What?"

"I saw his shoes," she whispered.

"Will you call the detective?"

"I don't know. I'll think about it."

She decided to cook dinner for Charley and herself. She opened cupboards and found a box of pasta, a large jar of sauce and a jar of peanut butter. In the fridge were the milk she had used, a jar of strawberry jam, a loaf of bread, a stick of butter, Italian salad dressing and a small plastic box of mixed greens. In one of the drawers was a bag of mandarin oranges. Should she use up Charley's food supplies?

She decided to call her and guessed she'd interrupted a meeting. Charley picked up and mumbled, "Is everything all right?"

"I was going to fix dinner. Is that okay? Didn't want to use up all your provisions."

"I'll bring dinner home. See you later."

Evie looked at her phone before putting it down. She couldn't do this every day. She needed her job. She still hadn't called the principal.

She opened her phone and scrolled through her contacts until she came to Jalinsky, took a deep breath and put in his number. It rang once.

"Detective Jalinsky."

She nearly hit the red hang-up.

"Hello," Jalinsky said again.

"Hello, Detective. This is…"

"I know who you are, Mrs. Harrington." His voice had softened. "I've been looking for you."

It dawned on her that the killer, if that's who he was, might be following him and Jalinsky might lead him to Charley's house. "Can we just talk on the phone?"

"Sure. Tell me what happened."

So, she did. She told Jalinsky what had happened and how she'd seen the man's shoes and bare ankles. He was stalking her, she realized.

"Do you think you're in a safe place now?" Jalinsky asked.

"Yes. That's why I don't think you should come over or we should meet. He might spot me, although he said I didn't know anything."

"Don't trust that," he said, sending shivers up her back.

"I can't hide forever," she said, hating herself for the plea in her voice.

"We're doing our best, Mrs. Harrington," he said. "Stay put a while longer."

"You mean don't go out?"

"Yes. That's exactly what I mean."

Wrapped up in the story she was reading, she identified with the mother. Only she wished the woman wasn't so proud. She hadn't heard the door open and was startled to see Charley enter the kitchen, carrying bags of groceries.

"So, I hope you like Chinese. I picked up a sweet and sour chicken and a broccoli thing and some crabmeat rangoons. We can share."

"I haven't had Chinese since forever." Bad grammar, she thought.

She watched Charley unload the bags. "So, can I cook tomorrow?"

"You can, but you don't have to."

"It's healthier." And she realized she had just insulted Charley. "I didn't mean that like it sounded." Of course, she had.

Charley smiled and lifted her eyebrows. "Yes, you did, and you're right. You can cook, only if you really want to."

"You don't like to cook?" Evie asked. Charley shook her head. "But you have this gorgeous kitchen."

"I know."

"I called Detective Jalinsky today. He talked like maybe it wouldn't be long till they catch this guy." Her voice faded when Charley's body came to attention.

"You what?"

"I thought he should know."

"You don't talk to the police unless I am with you, Evie. I thought I told you that."

"I guess I forgot."

Charley sighed and put her fork down. "You never talk to the police without an attorney at your side. You talk to me first."

"But you were busy."

"You're my client. I'm never busy for you." She stood up.

"Please don't stop eating. I'm sorry."

"I'm full," Charley said, but she sat down.

"I lost my appetite too." She put her fork down. She would chew Rebecca out royally, but she wouldn't snitch on her.

"Come on. Let's finish this." Charley forked a piece of broccoli. "Anything else happen today?"

"Rebecca stopped over."

"I'll bet it was good to have company."

"I won't talk to him again," Evie promised.

"Good."

They cleaned up together after eating, even though Evie said she'd do it. After all, Charley had been working all day.

Bedtime was awkward. Charley had said Evie should sleep with her until this was over, but she hadn't repeated it. Evie appeared in the doorway with her pajamas, pretending she was looking for Georgie.

"Have you seen him?"

"Last time I saw him he was in the kitchen. Why don't you go find him and come to bed? I hope you like to read a little. I do."

"I always read in bed," Evie said, heading for the kitchen. She carried Georgie back with her.

"Don't you think we should leave the door open in case he has to use the litter box?"

"I usually do." She'd panicked last night. She opened the book and soon she was crying, secretly trying to wipe her eyes and nose.

"Sad part?"

"Yeah. These kids intentionally hit the dog that was trying to protect his girl owner." She sniffed.

"Ah, *One Plus One*?"

"Don't tell me what happens," Evie said.

"I won't."

CHAPTER EIGHT

Evie slept without dreaming that night. She heard nothing, but she woke up to see Charley standing over her, scowling, with hands on hips. She was dressed in a suit.

"I fed Georgie."

"You don't have to." She wondered if that was the reason Charley looked upset.

"Evie, someone was in here last night."

Evie's heart froze and fear raced through her veins. "What? How do you know?" She pushed the covers back and got up. The clock read 6:48. "Do you always get up so early?"

"I can't leave you here."

She was surprised how disappointed she was. "I'll go home. I'll be fine." Would she?

"We have to move to a safe place. You need to pack and eat. I'll load the car. Thank God, it was in the garage last night."

A moment passed before Evie grasped what Charley had just told her. "A safe place? Where?"

"You'll see."

"Are you going to leave me there?" she asked, panicking.

"Pack some books. I don't know how long we'll be there."

"We?" She sounded like a dodo.

Before Charley went out the door, she turned. "You can't tell anyone where you are. You can't talk to anyone, not even Rebecca or Pam or your kids."

"But they'll worry, and they might report me missing."

"I'll take care of that." And Charley left the room.

Evie stood, stunned, for a minute or two. Then she got dressed, made the bed and began packing the clothes she had brought, which weren't many. She dressed in jeans and a sweatshirt and carried her overnight bag to the kitchen. Charley wasn't there, but there was coffee. She poured herself a cup and put a piece of bread in the toaster.

Charley reappeared and put a large cooler on the floor near the fridge. "Would you fill this when you're done eating? Leave a little milk and butter and bread in the refrigerator, enough so that it looks like someone lives here." She grabbed Evie's suitcase, pretending it was heavy. "Have you got any clothes in here or is it all books?" she asked with a grin before heading for the garage.

Evie smiled. She did as she'd been asked while she ate the toast and drank another cup of coffee. She packed a couple of grocery bags with bread and peanut butter and cereal and a few other things from the cupboards, leaving a few things behind.

Lastly, she carried out Georgie's things—his litter box and bag of litter, his food and bowls and kennel. She put on his harness and leash and led him to a Subaru wagon, which was parked on the other side of the Jeep.

"Are you ready?" Charley asked, eyeing the cat.

She watched as Evie sat in the front seat with the cat on her lap. Evie ran the seatbelt through the short vinyl belt attached to Georgie's halter and snapped it in place, so that they were both belted in. "Ready," she said.

"Who would have guessed?" Charley muttered, getting in behind the wheel. "Sure you have everything, because we're not coming back."

"Ever?" Evie asked.

"Not until this guy is caught."

"Don't you have to go to work?"

"I took some time off." The garage door went up and Charley drove out into sunshine and closed the door behind them. They drove toward Highway 10.

Evie checked her pockets for her phone. It wasn't there. She looked in her backpack that lay on the floor in front of her, which was difficult with Georgie on her lap. The phone wasn't there either. "I must has left it at the house." Evie looked pleadingly at Charley.

"I have it. I can't risk you calling or emailing anyone."

Incensed, Evie sputtered, "How could you? Where is it?"

"Why do you need it?"

"You're treating me like a child," Evie said stiffly, like a child might.

"There will be no service where we're going, no Wi-fi. Nothing. I'll give it to you when we get there. Okay?"

"No, it's not okay."

Charley reached into her pocket and placed the phone between them. "You can't forget this time. No calling anyone."

"But they'll worry."

Charley gave her a sharp look. "That's exactly why I had your phone. To protect you from your good intentions. If the killer traces us to this place, I'm out of options."

Evie picked up the phone and put it in her backpack. Knowing that Charley's intentions were meant to protect them didn't help. She bristled whenever someone took away her right to make her own decisions. But the day was golden. She opened her window a little, forgetting that Georgie didn't like a breeze. He squawked and she laughed, shutting the window. "Okay."

What was the point of being angry with Charley, who was taking her someplace where she'd be safe? "I'm sorry. How far away is this place?"

Charley gave her a dazzling smile before looking at the rearview mirror for the umpteenth time.

"Is someone following us?" she asked, fearfully.

"We're almost there. Just making sure no one is behind us." She flicked on her right blinker and pulled off the road. Cars zipped past them. Charley turned onto a dirt lane. After a few hundred feet, she stopped, reversed and backed behind a bunch of scrubby bushes and trees, disappearing from view.

"Do you do this with any other of your clients?" Evie asked.

Charley put a finger to her lips.

They waited in tense silence for what seemed like an hour but was only a few minutes. A battered F-150 pickup drove slowly past them. Charley jotted down something in a notebook as the truck vanished around a curve. After a few minutes, she started the Subaru, drove onto the highway and floored it. About a half hour later, she turned right onto the road to New London and after a quarter hour, flicked her right blinker, slowed for the car behind her to pass, then turned left onto a rutted lane covered with grass and small growth. The Subaru rocked and bounced. Georgie meowed as if miffed.

"Sorry, kitty. It won't be long now."

"That truck was following us?" Evie asked, running her hands nervously through her hair.

"Looked like it."

"I never saw the killer's vehicle," she muttered.

"Maybe whoever was in the truck had a place at the end of that dirt drive."

"Or found a place with people in it who didn't like trespassers."

Charley laughed. "Right."

"I'm tired of being terrorized." She glanced at Charley, whose hair was being lifted from her lovely neck by a breeze. Why was she even noticing Charley's neck? "And I dragged you into my nightmare."

"I came willingly. Think of it as an adventure."

"Who is going to take care of Georgie if something happens to me?"

"I will, unless something happens to me too."

"Hey, you're supposed to be reassuring me."

The car crawled through the tall grass. It brushed against the bottom of the vehicle.

Evie looked out her window. They were now driving above wetlands on one side and dense woods on the other. "Where are we going?"

"It won't be long now. You'll see."

About ten minutes later she caught sight of a small, wood-sided cabin, sitting on high ground. Charley parked in front of a wood porch, stacked with split logs. She got out, opened the back door and carried the cooler onto the porch. She unlocked the door to the cabin and strode inside.

Evie followed her, carrying Georgie. The place was very basic—an ancient refrigerator, a sagging countertop with a coffee pot and a two-burner gas stovetop. A pump with a handle sat next to a sink and open shelves above and below, filled with stained coffee cups, a variety of glasses, different-colored plates, a few bowls, odd size eating and cooking utensils, a Dutch oven and two fry pans. An old table with eight mismatched chairs stood near the kitchen stuff. On one wall were bunk beds. In the far corner was a potbelly stove and another room appeared to be behind a curtain.

Georgie was struggling to get down, so she stopped gawking and tied him to the leg of a chair before going to help unload the car. She brought in the kennel and stuffed the protesting cat into it and shut the door. Outside, the day was dying and cold was settling in. Steam rose off the wetlands. She looked around and saw narrow boardwalks going off in all directions.

She carried in her suitcase and backpack and went out for Georgie's things, putting them in his empty litter box and hurrying inside. Everywhere she went, she felt she was being watched. Was she paranoid or what? Charley was lighting kindling in the stove when she closed the door. "Is it okay to let Georgie out?"

"This stove is going to get red-hot. As long as he stays away from it, it's okay. Why don't you lock the door?"

She did so and began looking around the place. Behind the curtain was a room with a double bed, an old dresser and hooks on the wall. Overhead bulbs were the source of light. She asked about a toilet.

"There is a gas toilet. It burns the waste. It's behind that curtain near the stove. They use the same propane tank."

Georgie parked himself near the stove and Evie put his food and water and bed there. Then she put a leash on Georgie and went for a walk with Charley. It was a slow walk. The cat didn't like the gaps between the boards, so Evie picked him up.

"So, what is this place?"

"A hunting cabin." Charley pointed at a tree with a platform between limbs, high off the ground. "That's a tree stand for sighting game."

"Do you hunt?" She looked into Charley's eyes, which appeared to be very dark in the fading light.

"Not really. When I cried after shooting my first deer, my dad gave up on making me a hunter and concentrated on my brothers. My mother and I came out here in the spring and early fall. The mosquitoes will eat you alive if it's warm enough. Are you hungry?"

"Starved," Evie said.

They warmed up leftover chicken and mashed potatoes and Evie made a salad. They ate quietly, although Evie had at least ten questions she wanted to ask Charley. She decided to save them for later.

After cleaning up, they played a couple games of cribbage and went to bed. Georgie was already under the covers when they got there. They each had a book. Charley had fed the stove and trimmed and lit an old kerosene lantern before shutting off the overhead lights. The shades were drawn over the few windows.

The bed was small compared to a queen. Evie didn't have to scoot to be close enough to the light on Charley's bedstand to read. She opened *One Plus One* and began reading the part where someone helps the girl's mother take the dog to the vet, even though they couldn't afford the cost. She felt Charley looking at her.

She met the slate-blue eyes. "What? Am I too close?"

Charley smiled. "No. You're awfully pretty, Evie. You look a little like a gypsy with that black hair and those dark eyes. I was kind of jealous of you in high school."

Evie remembered Rebecca saying she looked like a gypsy, but the thought blipped by. "You, jealous of me? God, I thought you were like an Amazon when you ran up and down the basketball court, so coordinated and graceful, able to make a basket from midcourt."

Charley laughed. "Come on, Evie. I very seldom made a basket from midcourt. None of us did. I always thought it was nice of you to come and watch. We couldn't compete for an audience with the boys' team, although some of them watched, too." Charley took a breath and murmured, "Those were the glory days."

"I'll bet. Winning the English medal couldn't compete with sports."

"I was so impressed," Charley said. "I would have dated you if you'd been a boy."

"Yeah?" Evie asked, doubt in her voice.

"No, you're right. I would have dated you just as you are."

Evie blushed. She thought how Charley treated her a million times better than Ted ever had. "I wasn't brave enough to date you, but I would have loved to have been your friend."

Charley must have only heard the first half of the sentence, Evie thought, watching her slide down and turn toward her. She started to say, *No, No*, or did she just think it as she realized Charley was going to kiss her—on the lips.

How different and yet the same it was. Charley's lips were soft and pliant, and it seemed as if the kiss went on forever. She was pressed against Charley's soft breasts, but the rest of Charley was firm, like her arms, pulling Evie close. And the muscles in her back that Evie was caressing, or was she just exploring, were hard. Of course, she was taller than Evie. Her legs went on after Evie's ended.

Charley's hands moved through her hair, on her back, her breasts, between her legs. Evie froze.

"We better stop," Charley whispered. "This isn't in the rule book." But when Evie said nothing, her fingers slipped under the elastic of Evie's panties.

That was when Evie stopped thinking and began to respond. She moved against Charley's fingers, unable to stop herself. She plunged her hands into Charley's hair, down her back and into what Evie thought of as her private parts. She began to mimic what Charley was doing to her, because that was the only way she could keep from coming. Their hands were drenched, and Evie was astonished by how much this excited her. And then, unable to stop it, she lost control and came. She was panting. Every nerve was tingling, and Charley was moving fast against the pressure of her fingers until she, too, climaxed. Both convulsing at the end. Both breathing hard.

Charley kissed her again and put Evie's hand on her breast. Then she held Evie tight and whispered in her ear, "Thank you. I needed that."

Evie awoke disoriented in the morning with Georgie's whiskers in her face. She took a moment or so to figure out where she was before saying, "Okay, okay. I'll feed you, but first I have to pee." She got up, threw her long-sleeve nightshirt over her head, and walked out of the bedroom with the cat dancing excitedly in front of her. "I wish that was all I had to worry about," she said to his tail.

Charley was feeding wood onto the red cinders in the stove. She looked up and smiled as Evie hurried past. When she returned, Charley was poking the burning logs. The heat of the fire had turned her face red. She closed the door and went into the bedroom.

Evie fed the cat and followed Charley to get dressed. They looked at each other across the bed and climbed back in.

Evie had never had sex like this. Ted had often said, "Your pussy smells like fish." No matter that she had washed up beforehand. He'd touch her a few minutes and force himself inside. She knew from talking to Rebecca that all men were not like Ted, though.

Charley removed Evie's nightshirt and her own pajamas. She pulled Evie as close as possible, so that their warm skin touched wherever possible. She kissed Evie's eyelids, eyebrows, forehead, cheeks before covering her lips with her own. Their tongues met and Evie felt a gush of sticky wetness between her legs. Embarrassed, she squeezed them together.

Charley laughed and placed her hand there. "Lovemaking juice. Wouldn't be possible without it." She covered Evie's breast with that same hand, and Evie cringed, thinking that she wouldn't be able to shower afterward.

"We have a nice little tub. We'll put it in front of the stove and heat water to fill it," Charley said, as if she were reading Evie's mind.

Evie copied her—hand between the legs and on the breast. She breathed deeply and kissed Charley's breast. Her hand, which was near her nose, did not smell fishy. Before she realized what was happening, she felt Charley's tongue stroking, her fingers entering her, and she could do nothing about it. It was so exquisite that she lifted her hips in response.

Charley was above her, on her knees, and without thinking Evie pulled her down and tasted her too. It did not last long. The intense feeling climaxed quickly for Evie, followed in a matter of moments for Charley.

Charley rolled off Evie and scooped her into her arms. Neither said anything until Georgie jumped on the bed. They both laughed and Charley asked if Evie was ready for breakfast.

Evie couldn't resist. "I thought I just had breakfast."

CHAPTER NINE

The two women spent the day walking the boardwalks that spread out like arms from the cabin, taking turns carrying Georgie and watching water birds in the wetlands: hawks, ducks, and songbirds. Even a pair of otters showed up as if they were there for their entertainment.

Charley said the wetlands extended to the Wolf River. "When the water is high, which it is now, you can catch fish off the boardwalks. We might have to do that. We'll run out of food in a few days."

"Sooner than that." Evie had seen the inside of the fridge and cupboards.

"I should have planned this a little better," Charley said.

"No. It was so kind of you to bring me here." Evie looked her in the eyes. "How many people would put their lives in danger like you have?"

Charley's eyebrows arched and she grinned. "I really didn't have an ulterior motive."

"I'm supposed to believe that?"

Charley put her arm around Evie. "You know, I hate to say this, but we need to get you a new attorney."

"Why? I like my attorney."

"Because we can't make love if I'm your attorney. It's frowned upon. I could lose my job. Which would you rather have me be, your lover or your lawyer?"

"Both," Evie said. "And I should call Rebecca before she calls the police and says I'm missing. I'll swear her to secrecy."

"You'll be lucky to get a connection."

Evie pulled her phone out of her pocket and tried to establish a connection. Her phone kept repeating, *Emergency Calls Only*.

"Turn it off before you're hacked. Let's go back and stoke up the fire." The day was turning cool. "We'll go home tomorrow."

"I don't want to go home," Evie said. "If I could get hold of Rebecca, she would call off the cops."

"To do that we'd have to go someplace where they have Wi-fi, like a gas station. There's a Kwik Trip further down the road. It's a risk but they do have food."

When they got back to the cabin, Charley suggested they wait till after dark. "We'll all go. It's better we stick together."

Taut with fear, Evie looked at her. "That was him in that pickup, wasn't it?"

"I've never seen him, but I'd lay odds we were being followed." Her slate-blue eyes had turned dark with worry and her honey-blond hair was disheveled.

Evie wanted to bury her fingers in it. She stepped close and began to move pieces of hair around, and Charley put her arms around her and pulled her close.

"I could take you to bed again, but we need to eat and go to the gas station." She kissed Evie.

Georgie finished his food that evening, but neither woman did. When they got to the Kwik Trip, only one car was there. Charley pulled up next to a pump and started to fill up while Evie went inside. She picked up four oranges, two bananas, lettuce, coffee, cheese, milk, butter and bread, which she unloaded from a basket onto the counter. She figured they could have grilled cheese sandwiches and salad for a couple nights.

"You from around here?" the man behind the counter asked. "I haven't seen you before." He had hair halfway down his neck and a scruffy chin, as if he'd forgotten to shave. The name pinned to his shirt read *Tom*.

"I haven't seen you before either," Evie said.

"Two pretty girls like you shouldn't be out by yourselves."

"Who said we were by ourselves?" Charley asked and paid in twenties.

"Hey, nobody pays cash anymore," he said. "Don't you have a credit card?"

"Should we put the stuff back?" Charley asked.

He put the cash in the register drawer and gave Charley change, which she counted while he put the food in the cloth bags Charley had put on the counter.

They each grabbed the bags and the milk. "Thanks, Tom," Evie said as they went out the door.

"Quick, before he gets a good look at the car," Charley said and threw the bags inside.

Evie got in the front with the milk and they drove off. She watched the gas station in the side mirror before it disappeared. Tom had not come outside.

They went to bed as soon as Charley topped off the stove. The little cabin was warm, but the bed was warmer. They started over. Evie felt a little frantic and it must have shown because Charley whispered for her to slow down.

"I can't help thinking this might be the last time. I couldn't stand that. All my adult life I haven't had decent sex and now that I have, I don't want it to end."

"It's not going to end, Evie."

"You're not going to be my attorney, so when am I going to see you?"

"You're going to live with me," Charley said. "Now relax."

"I can't afford an attorney that charges five hundred an hour."

"We'll talk about that tomorrow. Okay?"

Charley covered Evie's mouth with her own and gave Evie's breast a gentle squeeze before placing a hand on her crotch. Her fingers burrowed through to the silky part and began moving slowly inside and out.

Evie stopped thinking and began to pay attention.

Charley grabbed her wrist and whispered, "Let's go down on each other. I want to taste you."

"I won't taste too good. I haven't had a shower since we got here." But she felt her body respond, and so did Charley, who gave a knowing laugh.

"You're wet enough. You'll taste good."

Of course, Evie came quickly, and Charley seemed to hurry to catch up. "I'm sorry. I'll get better. I just can't control myself." She was embarrassed.

"I love it. If you want to take a bath, we can heat up some water tomorrow."

"Can we both fit in the tub?"

At breakfast the next morning, famished from not eating the night before, they ate without speaking—an omelet and toast and of course, coffee. Evie was facing the window near the counter. The shade was pulled down, but a slash of light shone through. Something moved through the light, and she asked Charley if deer came near the cabin.

"Maybe when no one's around."

"Something walked through that little bit of sun outside the window."

Charley went to the window and moved the shade over. She came back to the table and quickly cleared it, putting the dishes in the sink. "Get your stuff together, Evie. We have to go."

Stunned, Evie asked, "What?"

"Get dressed and get Georgie ready." Charley was putting food back in the bags. Then she followed Evie into the bedroom and pulled her clothes on. "Hurry. We'll make one trip out to the car. Carry all we can. You'll have to take the cat and his stuff. I'll take my backpack and the food.

Evie stuffed clothes into the cat's kennel and put the cat on top of it with his halter and leash on. When they left, Charley quickly shut and locked the door, while Evie shoved the carrier into the back seat. Charley backed toward the car. With a shock, Evie saw the gun in her right hand.

"Get in!" Charley shouted. She threw the backpack in the back and jumped behind the wheel. She started the car and drove away. The vehicle bucked and rocked as Evie watched a man chasing them, yelling.

By the time they made it to the road, smoke was billowing into the sky from where the cabin had stood.

Charley said, "Call 911 and tell them someone set the cabin on fire at N1462, Highway 110." Tears ran down her face.

Evie's heart beat like crazy. All the way home she held Charley's hand or placed hers on Charley's leg, trying to comfort her. She had never felt so guilty in her life. She would go home, although the thought terrified her. It wasn't fair to put Charley at risk like this. She would tell Rebecca to come get her, since Evie's car was at her house.

In bed that night, Charley was inconsolable. Evie wrapped herself around her back and was relieved to feel Charley's hand on her arm. She thought Charley might not want her comfort, since what had happened was her fault.

The next morning before Charley left for work, she gave Evie the small handgun. Evie turned it over in her hand.

"I've never shot a gun. I've never wanted to shoot a gun." She tried to hand it back to Charley, who refused to take it.

"Aim, cock and shoot. I can't go anywhere if you don't take it and promise to use it to protect yourself."

So, she set it on the table. "Okay," she lied. As soon as Charley was gone, she called Rebecca.

"I want to go home," she said. "Would you come get me?"

"What happened?" Rebecca asked.

"I'll tell you later." She had no intention of telling her the truth.

"I can come around noon. Will that be all right?"

"Sure. I'll be ready." She didn't expect Charley home. She knew she had a lot of work to catch up on.

In the meantime, Evie unloaded the clothes from Georgie's kennel and stuffed them in her suitcase. She would wash them at home. Georgie was meowing in his kennel and everything else was packed and standing at the side door when Rebecca pulled into the driveway.

Evie opened the door and started piling her belongings onto the sidewalk before Rebecca got there. "Can you put Georgie in the car?" she asked without looking up.

"First tell me what's going on. You're not safe at home."

"Just help put the stuff in the car and then I'll tell you."

"Okay then, Georgie is not safe at home. Do you care about that?"

"Nobody is safe where I am," Evie said in a quivering, angry voice.

"Is that what this is all about? You don't want to put anyone else in danger. It's all right for you and Georgie to be in danger, but no one else?"

Evie saw Charley's car pull up beside Rebecca's. "Oh no. Now Charley's home. Why didn't you help me before she got here?" Evie looked away and began to cry.

"Hi, Rebecca. Shall we put Georgie and these other things inside and talk?"

Evie was livid. "Can't I live my own life the way I want?"

"You can, but please, let's talk about it first," Charley said in a calm voice, which made Evie even angrier.

Tears were dripping off her chin as she faced Rebecca and Charley. "Don't treat me like a child."

"We're not. Believe me. But don't you think you should have told me?" Charley asked.

Rebecca said, "Hey, girlfriend. Don't be angry. Don't be sad. You know I couldn't stand to lose you. You're my best friend."

Evie looked at Rebecca and laughed. "Who said anything about losing me?" Rebecca handed her a bedraggled tissue and Evie snatched it and wiped her nose and eyes. The three of them carried her belongings back into the condo.

Georgie sat meowing in his carrier. Rebecca looked at him. "Can I let him out?"

"I guess," Evie said, defeated, all her good intentions undone.

Charley was making coffee when Evie saw Rebecca staring at the table. The gun, she realized.

Rebecca raised a horrified face to Evie. "What in hell?"

"Ask Charley. It's her gun."

Charley turned slowly and said, "Guess I better put it away." She disappeared down the hallway with the weapon and was back before the other two had time to say anything. She filled three cups of coffee and put them on the table. "You might understand, Rebecca, if you heard about our two days away."

"I'm listening," Rebecca said, glancing at Evie.

Was it only two days? It seemed like longer and so much had happened.

Charley told the story, leaving out the sexual details. "There's no getting away from this guy. He apparently has an accomplice, and whatever they're looking for must be valuable. But we don't even know what it is. I left the weapon so that Evie would have something to protect herself with."

"Why were you leaving, Evie?" Charley asked.

"Because I can't put you at risk. Your childhood getaway was burned down because I was in it."

"Have you thought of calling Jalinsky?" Rebecca asked. "I think we need some reinforcements."

Charley said, "That's what I came home to talk to Evie about. I'm not comfortable leaving her alone."

"Call him. Go ahead," Evie said.

Charley got him on his cell and gave him her address. She asked if he could throw off any tail on his way over.

Evie heard him laugh. Rebecca looked at her and mouthed, "You had sex?"

"Not with Jalinsky," Evie murmured, making a face.

"No, I mean with her?" She pointed at Charley, who was getting more coffee while talking on the phone.

Evie nodded, just as Charley turned around and put her phone on the table. One side of her mouth lifted. "Can't keep anything from best friends, can you?"

Evie wondered if she looked as guilty as Rebecca.

"Let me share something with you. Remember Kelly, my teammate, my best friend? I know what the talk was about us in high school and university. It was true. But Kelly has been gone two years now, and I don't miss her." She looked from one to the other and said in a softer tone, "I really care about Evie."

At this unexpected confession both Evie and Rebecca looked nervous. The doorbell rang, silencing them. Evie was relieved because she had one of those uncontrollable urges to laugh. She could have howled at Rebecca's expression, but not in front of Charley.

CHAPTER TEN

Jalinsky took the offered cup of coffee from Charley. His cheeks were broad and his eyes narrow as if his background was Slavic, like his name. His bushy eyebrows contrasted with his gray, thinning hair. "Thanks," he said. "I parked a block over. I don't think anyone was behind me." He looked at the three women. "You're in over your heads, right?"

"Maybe," Charley admitted. "I'm a little worried."

"That was your hunting shack that was burned, Counselor?"

A flash of sorrow crossed Charley's face. "I should have known we were being followed."

"You're good. We lost you for a day. Did you know the gas station attendant was tied up in the back room? The guy you saw wasn't Tom."

"I guessed that," Charley said. "Who was he?"

"I don't know."

"Wait a minute. You were following us?" Evie said, struggling to catch up. "And the attendant at the Kwik Trip was one of the killers?"

"I don't know who he was. We haven't been able to identify them yet. This is a murder investigation. Until it's solved, you girls aren't safe."

"We're not girls," Evie said indignantly.

"Can you help us?" Charley asked Jalinsky.

"I've been trying." He turned to Evie. "What can you tell me about your husband?"

"A few years ago, he became secretive and sarcastic. It was after the kids left home. He'd be gone for a day or two, playing golf and going to meetings, or so he said. He'd never tell me where he went."

"You said he worked for Brighton Papers. He hasn't worked there in years."

Evie must have looked as surprised as she felt. "I called his secretary and she'd just say he was out of the office."

"Did he give you her number?"

"Well, yes," she said, feeling stupid. "I should have guessed."

"He was involved in hacking websites. I think he must have stashed away some of the profits."

"Why did they kill him when only he knew where the money was?"

"Maybe they didn't mean to kill him." Jalinsky shrugged. "I think your husband got in over his head and tried to get out and they didn't come to an agreement about how much money it would take. Or maybe they wanted it all."

"There really is more than one killer," Evie said. She wanted to cry. "I'd give them the money if I knew where it was."

Charley held up a hand. "Can I give him the golf sheet, Evie?"

"Sure. That's all I found."

Charley handed Jalinsky the piece of paper. He smoothed it out. "Where did you find this?"

Evie told him.

"Well, I'll see if I can find this golf course. Keep your heads down." He left, lighting a cigarette as he went out the door.

Rebecca stood. "I have a class in half an hour. I'll call you, Evie." She smiled at Charley and said goodbye.

Charley sat down next to Evie and looked into her eyes. She sighed. "If you left, Evie, I would worry terribly. I would also miss you terribly. I'd rather you stayed and we worked on this together."

Evie studied Charley's face. "You are so good-looking. You never called my name when you were a team captain in gym. Nobody wanted me or Rebecca to be on their team."

"Well, you and Rebecca were not exactly athletes. If I'd called on you, Kelly would have been jealous. I said you were awfully cute in front of her once, and she never forgot it. Anyway, it was like you and Rebecca were stuck to each other with Velcro. I thought you were in bed together."

Evie furrowed her black eyebrows and snapped, "What? You didn't pick me because of Kelly?"

"Listen to us. I don't want to think about high school. I long to take you to bed. I can't get you out of my head. Please, tell me you won't try to leave again."

"What about when my kids come home? Am I supposed to tell them they can't stay in the house where they grew up? That I can't stay there with them?" Evie met Charley's gaze.

"Tell them they can't come home, not yet. Now I must go to work. I'll be back around six. Please don't leave, and stay away from windows and doors."

"You're scaring me, you know?" Her heart had jumped into high gear.

"It's good to be a little scared." Charley kissed her and headed toward the garage door.

Left with nothing to do until it was time to make dinner, Evie found a mop and bucket in a closet and cleaned the kitchen. She sprayed the counters and washed the sinks and floor, and retired to the den to read. But the den reminded her of her own den where Ted had died, which brought to mind how dirty her house must be. She should be cleaning that house.

Instead, she lay down on Charley's bed and read *The Paris Architect*, a story about a French architect in occupied France during WWII, one who designed hiding places for Jews. It made her sick with worry. And she became angry with the men who were stalking her. And angry with Ted for causing all this trouble, even angry with him for dying. He got into this mess and died and dumped it on her.

The phone rang. She didn't recognize the Caller ID, so she didn't answer. Her cell, which was lying next to her, rang shortly after the landline silenced. She looked at the Caller ID. Same as the landline, so she answered.

"Hello?"

"This is Clarisse. I need to talk to Ted Harrington. Somebody keeps breaking into my house, looking for something he thinks is hidden here."

"Ted is dead. Someone killed him, maybe the same someone who is breaking into your place." She paused and heard breathing.

"Jesus," the woman said. "I'm as good as dead." She began to sob.

"Where do you live?"

"In the Villages in Florida."

"Why don't you call the police. Ted died here in Wisconsin, so it's probably not his killer."

"Who are you?"

"Ted's wife. He wasn't worth crying over. What's your last name anyway?" The woman hung up and Evie lay back on the pillow. "That son of a bitch," she said aloud. "Screwing around on me."

Charley didn't get home until seven. She looked so tired that Evie hadn't the heart to be upset, although dinner had been ready since five thirty. It was waiting in the fridge and Evie got it out and put it in the microwave. She dressed the salads and set them on the table.

"Are you hungry?" she asked.

"Starved," Charley said, but she didn't eat like she was famished. She played with her food. "I have to be in court the next two days."

"Okay," Evie said.

"It means I have to prepare tonight."

"Okay."

"I know you've been alone most of the day. I'm sorry."

"I realize you have to work, Charley. I don't have to be entertained."

Charley took a deep breath and began to wolf the salad down.

Evie took their plates out of the microwave and put them on the table. "It may be kind of dry by now."

"Sorry. I had a meeting and they dropped this case in my lap."

"Oh." Evie took a bite. It was a bit dry but still good, she thought. "Clarisse called me today."

"Should I know Clarisse?" Charley took a bite of the Mexican meatloaf. "It is good. Thanks."

"I don't know Clarisse, but she knew Ted. Someone has been breaking into her house in the Villages. She wanted to know where Ted was. When I told her he was murdered, she cried out that she was as good as dead. I told her to call the police."

Charley stared at her. "He had another woman?"

"Looks like it. Poor woman. I don't know why I answered." She ate a bit of garlic mashed potatoes.

"These are good. Garlic?"

"And milk and butter."

"You are a good cook, Evie."

She thought of Dave. He would be a great chef. She cleaned up the dishes and went to bed alone while Charley worked in her home office. She fell asleep before Charley came to bed, and when she awoke in the morning, Charley was gone. She left a note on the kitchen table:

Sorry, Evie. I'm hoping to be home at a decent hour and then we'll spend time together. Love, C

Evie decided to make a special dinner, perhaps shrimp pasta and a green salad with sweet peppers, onions, caramelized nuts, her special dressing and a good wine. But she'd have to go to the store to get some of the ingredients. She should go early when no one would be watching her. She could drive there in the Jeep and slip in and out of the store, but she had to go soon.

She dressed, fed the cat, and ate a bowl of cereal while writing her list. She felt as if she'd been freed from jail as she drove through morning traffic. She wasn't doing well with being stuck inside.

A horn sounded behind her and she stepped on the gas without looking and nearly rear-ended the car in front of her. The light was green but the line was long. Vehicles peeled away from her as she made her way to Woodman's. At this hour on a weekday, the parking lot was half full. The air smelled wonderful, and birds were singing as she hurried into the grocery store. The doors slid shut behind her and the familiar smells of shopping filled her nostrils. She actually liked planning meals and grocery shopping. She didn't linger long, though. Zipping up and down aisles, she purchased what was needed and checked herself out. She never went through a regular checkout counter anymore.

She loaded her groceries in the back of the Jeep, went to put the cart away, and felt something hard between her shoulder blades. "Leave it and come with me," said a familiar voice. It was him! Her legs nearly collapsed under her. She ran toward the doors, waving her arms in the air and screaming.

"Hey, hey, honey, what's the matter?" an older man asked as the automatic doors slid closed behind them.

"Run," she yelled, pulling on his sleeve and the doors opened again.

Two bullets slammed into the wall just behind them as the second set of doors slid shut. Evie kept running right in front of the man. When she stopped at the liquor checkout counter, she was breathless, and the man was gone. Out of the corner of her eye, she saw the same doors they had come through close behind him.

"What's wrong?" the young man behind the counter asked.

"He's one of them," she nearly shouted. "The other shot at me."

"Calm down," the clerk said.

She shook her head violently. "Call the police. Ask for Detective Jalinsky."

He called the store manager and then Jalinsky. When his boss arrived, both stared at her. "The detective is on his way," the clerk said.

"Where are these bullets?" the manager asked.

"Out there in the area between the doors," she said, waving frantically. She thought her heart would explode. "Don't go there!"

"We need to block that area off," he said and left them.

"Sit down," the clerk said to Evie, pointing at the bench near the door.

"He tried to kill me." It was just sinking in. How foolish she was to come to the store. She wondered if they knew where she was staying.

And then, so swiftly that she could hardly believe it, there were cops everywhere. But, of course, the men who had accosted her were gone. Jalinsky sat next to her and listened as she told him what had happened.

"He's going to kill me," she said.

"You have to stay put. You can't go places like you used to."

"He probably knows where I'm living." She stared at him, willing him to say no.

He sighed. "I don't know."

He drove her car to Charley's condo with a cop following. They turned onto side streets, parked in lots and watched for a tail to drive past. Finally, he pulled into Charley's garage and shut the door behind them. He helped her carry the groceries inside, making small talk, perhaps to set her at ease.

"Looks like it's going to be a good meal," he said. "Shrimp something?"

"Pasta. Shrimp pasta and salad and baked bread. Want to stay?" Move in with us, she wanted to say.

"Do you have any relatives from out-of-state?" he asked when the groceries were put away.

"No, not anyone I could stay with. Ted put them all off me. He told them I said terrible things about them. Not true, but they believed him." She'd been so naïve. She hadn't even known she was married to a control freak.

Before Jalinsky left, he handed her a card with his name and number. "Don't hesitate to call. But don't go out either. If you need something, call me. I'll send someone to go get it. Lock the doors and windows. Talk to your friends on a landline." And then he was gone.

She put the card in her pocket. They already had one magnetized to the fridge. She looked at her watch and called Pam. Maybe she would be home. Rebecca wouldn't.

"I wasn't sure where you were. I should have called. Anything happening?"

Evie told her about her trip to the store.

"So that was you. It's on the news. Should I bring Max over to stay with you during the day?"

She remembered how the dog had whined for Pam, and then she realized that Pam might be followed. She told her thanks but no and why. After she hung up, she called Rebecca and left a message that she shouldn't come over.

Five minutes later, Rebecca called. "I heard the news. Was that you they were talking about?" She sounded horrified.

"Yes. They're going to follow you to find out where I'm staying. Better for both of us if you stay away."

"I can't bear this," Rebecca said.

"I know." She heard the garage door open, and her hair stood on end. "I'll call you back."

Charley wrapped her in an embrace, and Evie cried into her suit jacket.

CHAPTER ELEVEN

She snuggled against Charley that night. It was comforting if not exactly comfortable—legs entwined, bodily sweat sealing them together, arms crossed over each other. Evie knew she could never sleep this way.

She let go and rolled onto her back, but a few minutes later she was pressed against Charley again. Charley rolled over and took Evie into her arms. "Look, let's lie side by side as close as we can get. That will work, won't it?"

They fell asleep hip to hip, shoulder to shoulder. It was the tenseness in Charley that woke Evie a few hours later. Someone was in the condo. Charley put a finger against Evie's lips and pushed her down when she started to get up on her elbows. There were footsteps in the hall.

They padded past their bedroom door and into the guest room where Evie's suitcase lay. They could hear rustling, as if pockets were being investigated and the sound of drawers being slid open and the faint rustling again. Charley slowly slid out of bed. Evie could see the outline of the gun in her hand. She padded to the door. Evie's heart was beating so loudly she was sure the intruder could hear it.

She started to get up and Charley waved her back. Suddenly her hand shot out and she said, "Stop right there. I'm a good shot, and no way could I miss this close." She edged out the doorway. "Get in the kitchen. Go on. Evie, call Jalinsky, will you?"

With shaking hands Evie made the call on her cell phone. It rang four times before Jalinsky picked up.

"Yeah? Who is this anyway?"

"It's Evie," she stammered. "Someone broke into the condo. Can you send one of your guys to get him? Charley has a gun on him."

"I'm pulling on my pants. Be there in ten minutes. Tell Charley not to get trigger-happy."

"She'll shoot him rather than let him get away."

She put a robe on and carried one out to Charley. The man was someone she'd never seen before. Middle-aged and skinny with sallow skin, like a night creature who never saw the sun.

"Can I have a drink of water?" he asked in a squeaky voice.

"No, you can't have a drink of water," Charley said.

"I'm thirsty," he whined.

"When the cops get here, you can ask them." She slid the robe on without taking the gun off the man.

"What kind of bitch are you?"

"Shut your mouth," Charley said. "If you open it again, I'll shoot you."

He started to get up and Charley hit him over the head with the butt of the gun. He slumped in the chair. "Where the fuck is Jalinsky?" she asked.

Evie stared at Charley with alarm. "He's coming."

Someone banged on the front door and the intruder leaped to his feet. The gun went off, making Evie jump, and the stranger fell to the floor and grabbed his foot. Blood spurted on the kitchen tiles, turning their pale pink color into bright red.

"You shot me!"

"And I'll shoot you again if you get up. Next time maybe I'll aim for your balls."

Evie ran to the door and peeked through the peephole before jerking it open. "In the kitchen," she said, wondering why he was alone. Why there weren't any other cops.

Jalinsky's gray hair stood on end. He probably had just gotten out of bed and thrown on yesterday's clothes. He jerked the intruder to his feet and the man howled. "You got anything to wrap that with?" He nodded toward the bloody wound.

"In the bathroom closet, Evie."

Evie came back with a box of gauze and medical tape. Jalinsky wrapped the foot, not too gently. The man yelled in pain, and Evie cringed. It hurt to watch.

Jalinsky dragged him out the door.

"God, he's so mean," Evie said of the cop.

"That guy probably would've killed you without a second thought," Charley said, looking at her. "Don't be a softie, Evie. Whoever is breaking in doesn't care whether either of us lives or dies. He's after something that you have."

"I don't know what it is," Evie said in a loud, frustrated voice. "I'd give it to them." Feeling alarmed, she said, "I think there's more than one guy."

"No shit!" Charley said.

"I don't know what to do," she whispered.

"Let's go back to bed. We can talk about it there."

Charley held Evie in her arms and even started a caress, but she fell asleep before completing it, her arm lying heavily on Evie as her breathing evened out.

Evie removed the arm and rolled onto her side, embracing the cat instead. Georgie clung to her like Velcro. He was a comfort. Soft and furry, a purr vibrating from within. She sighed, too alarmed to sleep at first. Slowly, it overcame her—the soft darkness, blurring everything.

There was never time in the morning for much discussion, especially this morning when they'd overslept and breakfast was hurried. Instead, they argued. It was Saturday and Charley had to work.

"I can't stay in all the time anymore," Evie said. "I want to see Rebecca and Pam. I want to take Georgie for a walk. That's not asking for much."

"No, it's not. But you can't do it. Someone is probably watching."

"You know what? I don't care anymore."

"You care about Rebecca and Pam, don't you?"

"I need fresh air and sunshine."

"Call them on the landline if you have to," Charley said, throwing her napkin on the table as she pushed her chair back and stood. They'd had the taps removed from the phones, but the guy last night could have put them back on.

"Can't Rebecca come over?"

"If she parks on another block, maybe. It's risky, though." She looked down at Evie and then put a hand on her shoulder. "Look. I'm sorry. I'm worried."

"I've been grown up as long as you have," Evie said, realizing how childish she sounded, but unable to just shut up.

"I'll see you early afternoon." Charley headed for the garage.

As soon as she was gone, Evie felt the shame. What was the matter with her? She had cabin fever, big time, and she didn't like being told what not to do. "Fuck." She slammed her chair back under the table. Georgie bolted and she ran after him, telling him she was sorry. She hadn't meant to scare him. The doorbell rang and she carried the cat with her. He jumped to the floor as she looked through the peephole.

With joy, she yanked the door open. "Rebecca. Come in. Quick." She slammed the door shut after her, locking it.

Rebecca wrapped her arms around her and pulled her close. "I miss you so much. How have you been?" She held Evie at arm's length. "You look tired."

"Somebody broke in last night," Evie said and told her the story, watching the horror grow on Rebecca's face. "I called Jalinsky, and he came and took him away but not before Charley shot the guy in the foot. He tried to get up after she told him not to."

Rebecca covered her mouth. "Oh, my God. How do you stand it?"

"I don't think it was the same guy who broke into my house or the one who burned down Charley's hunting shack." Then she felt guilty about calling the place a shack, but that's what it was. "Don't tell Charley I called her getaway a shack. She'd be so hurt."

"I won't."

"Let's go in the kitchen. I'll put the coffee on."

"Where's Charley?" Rebecca asked as they walked through the dark living room, where they no longer opened the drapes.

"At work. She's always at work. And I can't go anywhere." She started a new pot of decaffeinated coffee.

Rebecca cleared the table, rinsing and putting the breakfast dishes in the dishwasher. She slid a cloth bag off her shoulder and put it on the floor. "Books for you."

"Thanks, Rebecca. Just what I need to keep me occupied." Evie wiped the table clean. "Sit down." She knew Rebecca would want to talk about her relationship with Charley. They hadn't had a chance to do that.

They looked across the table at each other, almost shyly. "How's life?" Evie asked, before remembering. She gasped. "Where did you park?"

"Four blocks away. I didn't see anyone walking over. My life is same-old. Work, shop, home, garden."

"See, that's just it. I can't go outside and it's so nice out."

"What's it like living with Charley? What is she like? Or am I being too nosy? I always admired her athleticism because I suck at sports. I always thought she'd play professionally, and instead, she's an attorney."

"Yeah, I know. She's one of those people that make you feel inferior." And then she felt guilty. What kind of a person was she anyway? Charley had taken her in, had even shot someone in her cause, and she was Evie's pro bono lawyer until they found another. By now, Evie wasn't sure anyone thought she'd killed Ted.

"You don't love her?" Rebecca asked.

"I do. But I want to go back to my old life. I'm thinking about renewing my teacher's license online, but everything is so out of control." She thought of the little kids pulling on her clothes, holding her hands, talking to her, wanting to eat lunch with her, asking her to push them on the swing. Telling her she looked like their grandma, that she could be their grandma. They were worth the trouble.

"I think you should probably wait till this is all over. I took a course online. Remember? All I did was complain." Rebecca looked so serious. "It was difficult."

"Charley says they're watching." Chills raced down her spine. She glanced at Rebecca through the steam of her coffee and suddenly felt the urge to laugh. "I'm an ingrate, aren't I?"

Rebecca nodded and giggled. The giggles turned into laughter and before long they were both howling.

Evie was in pain. She couldn't talk. It was like the laughter of their younger days when they went into uncontrollable fits of merriment over almost nothing. Finally getting herself under control, she was afraid to meet Rebecca's gaze. It would set them off again.

When she did look, Rebecca was wiping her eyes with a napkin. "That felt good. Painful but freeing."

They began to talk with ease. Rebecca asked, "What's it like to be with a woman?" She put up her palms. "You don't have to answer that."

"You've been dying to ask, haven't you?" Evie grinned. "It's good, but Ted was a terrible lover. I have no comparison except that kid in college and he'd come if I touched him." She gave Rebecca a shy smile. "That's what you wanted to know, right?"

"I was just asking in general. Who cooks, who cleans, that sort of thing."

"Yeah, yeah. I know you." She sobered. "Charley's a wonderful lover, but then she's good at everything." Evie got up to fill their cups. "Except cooking. I've got her beat there."

"Is that how it is? Are you always trying to best each other?"

Were they? Evie wondered. She'd have to think about that one. "Have you seen Pam and Max?"

"She left you this." Rebecca fished a folded piece of paper out of her purse and placed it on the table. "Put her place up for sale and moved back home."

"Because she was afraid, I suppose." She opened the paper and smoothed it out. "I liked her." A couple of tears fell as she read the few lines, saying how sorry she was that she wouldn't see Evie before she left. How she hoped everything would be okay, that they would find the killer. She would look for it in the newspaper. She would call when that happened. She had included her cell phone number, which Evie already knew.

"I liked her, too."

They talked about their children and Rebecca's husband, John.

"How am I going to tell my daughter I'm living with a woman, Rebecca?" Evie asked with sudden alarm. "Dave will understand but Angie won't. Poor girl. She'll be so disillusioned."

"You could tell her this is a safe haven. You don't have to tell her anything more. Not yet anyway."

"I haven't talked to either one of my kids, except for a few words, since they were home. Now they can't come home. One of my greatest fears is that one of them will be kidnapped by those creeps to get me to tell them what they want. I don't even know what they want."

Rebecca sat up straight. "It's probably drugs."

Her voice dropped. "He must have hidden something valuable somewhere, and they think I know where. They've had time to tear up the house looking by now. Even if it's true, Ted would never have told me."

"Listen, Evie. If Angie and Dave do want to come home, they can stay with me. Okay? You don't want them at your house."

"No. Dave could stay here. I don't know if Angie would want to. Anyway, she's working. Dave would normally come home at the end of the spring semester and get a job."

That would be the end of hiding her relationship with Charley. The end of hiding, period. But she didn't think Dave would tell anyone.

As if Rebecca was reading her mind, she said, "You don't want anyone finding out where you are. Dave can stay with me."

Evie heard the garage door open. Charley was home. "Where did the time go?"

Rebecca stood up. "I better leave."

"You better not," Evie shot back. "Stay for lunch. Please, Rebecca."

Charley's face was a perfect picture of surprise. She recovered quickly, though. "Hi, Rebecca. So good to see you." She set her briefcase down against the doorframe and kicked off her heels.

Rebecca smiled. "So surprised to see me. I couldn't stay away any longer."

"Nor should you. Where did you park?"

"A few blocks away on Clark Street."

"We'll have leftovers," Evie said, abruptly standing.

"Don't do anything special for me. I love peanut butter and jelly sandwiches," Rebecca said.

"What's new, Rebecca?" Charley asked, her eyebrows arching in question.

"I've been teaching a couple of math classes at Tech. The students aren't all kids, you know. Some are older. I like it." She looked at Evie. "The sooner you get your license, Evie, the better. The kids love you."

Evie said, "I will when all this is over."

"God, I wish I taught something," Charley said. "I'd like to have a forty-hour week."

"Well, you could teach law and have a sixty-hour week," Rebecca said with a smile. "Or you could go into politics."

"And never have a private life."

"I would divorce you," Evie said, and they all laughed.

After lunch, Charley said, "I'm sorry there wasn't a chance to break this to you first, Evie. I'm glad Rebecca is here, though, because she needs to hear this too."

Uh oh, Evie thought. Now what?

"We're going away for a few weeks. I won't tell Rebecca where, even though I think we can trust her to not tell anyone anything. But I don't want her to have to lie."

"Last time we went away someone burned down your getaway," Evie pointed out.

"I know, but I doubt anyone will find us this time."

"What about my kids?" Evie asked.

Rebecca said, "If they can't find you, they'll call me. I'll say the house is part of the investigation, but they can stay with me. I'll say you're on vacation, but you didn't tell me where you're going."

"They won't believe you."

Charley said, "We're not telling anyone else anything."

"Not even Jalinsky?" Evie asked.

"Especially not Jalinsky. No one. No police. No friends or family members. Only Rebecca." Her eyes met Rebecca's. "Can you fend them off?"

"I can always plead ignorance."

Rebecca hugged Evie extra tight at the door. "Be safe. Have fun. I'll miss you."

"I'll miss you, too. You'll be the first person I call when I get back." That she was going away without even telling her kids made her feel a teeny bit guilty. Oh, well. Angie had called her from Florida last winter.

"Surprise," she had shouted in drunken joy.

"Why surprise?" she had asked.

"I'm on the beach on Siesta Key. It's heaven."

"You're supposed to tell me when you go somewhere," she'd said, exasperated.

"I told Dad. He gave me the money."

Figures, she'd thought. He never told her anything anymore.

CHAPTER TWELVE

"Where and when?" Evie looked into Charley's slate-blue eyes and felt a twinge of desire.

Charley smiled as if she could tell what Evie was feeling. "Tonight."

"Where?" Evie turned to walk away and Charley pulled her back.

"You'll like it," she whispered in Evie's ear, and the hair stood up on Evie's neck. "Go pack your suitcase."

"How long will we be gone?"

"Cram as many shorts and T-shirts and undies as you can into your suitcase. Oh, and don't forget a swimsuit and shampoo and suntan lotion and sandals and your Kindle."

So, there would be electricity. She scrounged around in the bag of clothes she had brought from her house and made a wrinkled pile on the bed. She thought she should wash and iron them, but Charley said there wasn't time.

"We're going to eat dinner, clean up the dishes and leave as soon as it's dark. Wear an old pair of jeans, a long-sleeve shirt, tennis shoes and a light jacket, sweatshirt or both."

Evie questioned her but got no answers. She went to the kitchen, wishing they hadn't eaten the leftovers. "We'll just have lunch, since we already ate dinner," she said aloud to herself. She made grilled cheese sandwiches, which they ate while listening to *All Things Considered*.

Charley swallowed the last of her sandwich. "I'll put the bags in the car." She went down the hall to the guest room where Evie kept her clothes. Both were dressed in jeans. Evie wore her long-sleeve Wisconsin shirt and white tennis shoes. She was taking the zip-up Wisconsin sweatshirt and the light jacket that hung on the back of her chair. She cleaned the dishes and turned off the radio. She hadn't been able to concentrate on the news anyway. She was so excited.

Charley came in from the garage. "What do you have in that bag? It's so heavy."

The phone rang, startling Evie.

"Don't answer," Charley said. "Time for one last tinkle. Then we leave."

When Evie reached for the light switch before they went out the door, Charley grabbed her hand. "Leave it on." Then she turned on the TV and a couple of lamps in the den.

Charley backed the Jeep out of the garage, shutting the overhead door. She switched on the headlights when they reached the corner.

When they turned onto College Avenue, Evie asked, "Are we going to the airport?"

"Sort of," Charley said, checking the mirrors constantly.

"Are we being followed?" Evie asked, beginning to look around, her heart picking up speed.

"Don't think so."

Charley turned into the area with the private planes instead of the international airport. "Be ready to grab your bag and follow me."

This is like a movie, Evie thought, as she jumped out of the Jeep, grabbed her bag and hurried after Charley.

They climbed the portable steps and ducked into a small, sleek jet. A tall, broad-shouldered man with thick brown hair stood just inside. "Welcome," he said and pulled the door shut after them, while outside another man wheeled away the steps. "Find a seat and fasten your seatbelts."

They took seats across the narrow aisle from each other, and Charley introduced the man now leaning from the bulkhead. "Evie, our pilot is my brother, Jeremy."

He looked faintly amused and dipped his head at Evie. "Welcome aboard. Fasten your seatbelts. Sit tight. It's only a four-hour flight."

"Hi," Evie said, glad she had her Kindle.

"When the seatbelt light goes off, you can get food out of the fridge. You can even make coffee, but you have to bring me a cup. No one else is on the plane."

Evie looked out her window as the engines revved. She held her breath until they were in the air, then watched as the city fell away. The night was filled with stars. As they flew south, or what she thought was south, the lights became one long string.

She opened her Kindle and read a few pages before falling asleep. In a dream, a strange person was trying to make her eat something that looked horrid. She opened her eyes and saw Charley bending over her, balancing a cup of hot chocolate. She put it in the cup holder.

"Sorry I woke you up," she said.

"I love hot chocolate. Thanks." She looked out the window. The strings of light were gone. "Where are we going?"

"To a private key. A barrier island. My boss owns it."

"Why would your boss let you off work and send us to his private island?"

"Because he's my dad."

"A family affair," Evie said. She didn't want to be beholden to people she didn't even know.

"Well, yes and no."

"What does that mean?"

"It means he's got a reason, an ulterior motive. You're just a happy by-product."

"Can you tell me the reason?"

Charley looked at her and said quietly, "No. I'm sorry."

"Is Jeremy staying with us on the island?"

"Nope. It will be just you and me."

Evie sipped her hot chocolate to hide her smile. It sounded like something out of a dream.

* * *

They came to a bumpy landing on a small strip at a tiny airport and braked to a hair-raising stop near a hangar with three airplanes parked nearby.

A silver car headed toward them as the engines stopped. A man jumped out of it and began pushing stairs toward the plane. Charley got up and removed their luggage from the small overhead bin.

Evie grabbed her bag, put the Kindle in the side pocket and followed Charley to the door, where the stairs were being put in place. Charley stood on her toes and kissed Jeremy's cheek, while Evie thanked him. The man took the bags and put them in a silver Ford Escape.

He too got a kiss from Charley before she and Evie climbed into the front seat of the Escape. The man was already wheeling the stairs back to the hangar. Then he grinned and ran toward the jet, leaped in the air and grabbed the molding around the open door. With Jeremy helping, he climbed into the jet, while Evie watched with an open mouth.

As Charley drove toward the road, the small jet began bumping back to the runway. Its engines revved and it sped down the strip of concrete and lifted into the air. Overhead, the jet tilted its wings and flew away.

"Let me guess. Another brother?" Evie asked.

"Yup. Tony. He and Jeremy are twins. They've been practicing that move since they were teenagers."

The private jet and the private island made Evie realize how different her own upbringing had been. "Why didn't you go to a private school?" she asked as they merged into traffic.

"I didn't want to. I wanted to go to the same school as my best friend."

"Kelly Longstadt?" she said. Of course, she knew. They all knew.

Charley shot her a look. "Yes."

"What happened to her?"

Charley looked in her mirrors and changed lanes. "We're going to get off soon."

Evie glanced at her surroundings. Maybe she needed to know where she was. They whizzed past signs with gas stations on one side and food places on the other and eased onto an exit ramp. At the stop light, they turned left and drove a few blocks to a parking space under a building.

"Almost there," Charley said.

Too surprised to ask questions, Evie grabbed both bags while Charley checked the interior of the car and locked it. She gave Charley her bag and they walked down an access road toward the Gulf. It rolled toward them, each wave receding as the next one crashed onto the beach. The sun was shining. A soft breeze off the water brought cool air. How could Evie feel anything but excitement and anticipation?

The two women stepped onto a dock with cabin cruisers tied to berths. They stopped at one much like the others, rocking against its lines. Charley threw her bag into the boat and took Evie's and did the same. She stepped gracefully onboard and reached for Evie's hand and helped her safely aboard. Together, they released the lines holding the boat and threw them onto the dock.

Charley backed the cruiser out of its berth and turned it toward an island that she said was almost five miles offshore. When she passed the end of the dock, she pushed the boat to full throttle, a wide grin plastered across her face. Pinned to the bench seat at the back of the boat, her eyes half-closed by wind, Evie was thrilled.

Charley drove around the island. It was long and narrow with trees growing down to the beach that encircled it. A bungalow had been built on the highest point. Charley eased the craft next to a small dock and grabbed a line.

They snugged the large boat to the bumpers attached to the dock and began to unload. Evie was surprised to see net bags with food in them. A small fridge held perishables. Together they carried the food and their bags to the bungalow in four trips. Charley turned on the electricity and water and they loaded food into the fridge and cabinets.

Evie walked around the bungalow—three small bedrooms, a kitchen, a living room with a screened-in lanai off it. Windows all around. Tile floors. A small TV in the living room. A lap pool next to the lanai.

Charley came up from behind and wrapped her arms around Evie. "How do you like it?"

Evie always melted inside when she did this. "I can hardly believe it. I mean, getting here was like being in a movie."

"My brothers would be pleased to hear that. Why don't we put on our swimsuits and enjoy the rest of the day?"

They changed in the bedroom but were distracted in the process. Just as Evie was stepping into her suit, Charley came around the bed. "Don't put it on just yet."

"Why?" she asked stupidly. She met Charley's eyes, darkened by desire, and laughed. "I should have guessed, but it's so nice out. You could cool off in the water." She was teasing.

Charley let out a growl, picked her up and laid her on the bed.

"Doesn't look like I have a choice."

"Yes, you do." She backed off and Evie reached for her.

"Just kidding."

Making love while bathed in sun coming through the window, along with a warm breeze, enhanced the experience. Every nerve tingled. Goose bumps covered Evie's skin. She closed her eyes, feeling so alive, and let the sensations take over. Evie knew she wasn't as good a lover as Charley, that Charley orchestrated their lovemaking. Partly because she lost control under Charley's touch but mostly because Charley was more skilled.

After, they walked into the cool water to wash the stickiness away. Evie was afraid of the creatures in the Gulf. She thought any minute a shark would attack her, so she splashed onto the beach while Charley floated on her back.

The beach looked white from a distance, but up close it was a light color, the sand cool and soft against her feet. She walked along, looking for shells washed in on the tide. When Charley caught up to her, both of Evie's hands were full.

"Such a great pastime. I'll go get a couple of chairs and a bag for your shells."

"I'll come with you." She couldn't be on the beach without a book.

Charley looked out at the water and frowned. A speedboat was idling offshore. She pointed to the sign at the end of the dock that read, NO TRESPASSING.

"Aw, come on," one of the three guys in the boat yelled. "You can't keep an entire island to yourself."

A boat with two men in it sped around the end of the island and drove up to the offending one.

Evie watched this exchange with worry. "What if the guys come back at night," she asked.

"The men in the speedboat come ashore at night. It's so annoying that we even have to hire them."

The intruding boat slowly motored away, the young men greedily eyeing the women. Evie wanted to wrap herself in a beach towel but there was none. She felt so exposed.

Both went inside where they picked up something to read and a couple of beach towels. Charley found Evie a bag. Outside, Evie followed Charley to a storage shed near the house where they grabbed a couple of beach chairs. When they returned to the beach, there were no boats offshore.

It was heaven, Evie thought, smearing herself and Charley with sunscreen. She read a little before resting her head on the back of the chair and falling asleep.

Charley woke her with hummus and chips and two glasses on a tray. "How about a little snack and a drink?"

Evie sat up and sipped the vodka and tonic. It was ice cold. She squeezed the quarter piece of lime over the liquid and drank again. "Yum. Thank you."

"Welcome," Charley said with a crooked grin.

"What?" she asked, digging her toes into the cool sand.

"It's just so nice to have you here."

"It's incredible to be here. Thank you."

Charley nodded and Evie thought this was a good time to ask about what happened to Kelly. Would she come back and take Evie's place?

"What are you thinking?" Charley asked, giving Evie the perfect opening.

"I was wondering what happened to Kelly Longstadt." She could picture Kelly and Charley, ponytails flying, dribbling up and down the high school gym floor, passing the ball back and forth between them.

Charley frowned. "It didn't work out. She met someone new and more exciting. An attorney was too stodgy."

"But didn't she have to work?"

"She didn't want to work, but I had to. We couldn't travel all the time."

Evie was quiet for a moment, thinking about this. "But we're here at this gorgeous place. You're not working."

Charley smiled that sexy grin. "In a way, I am. Keeping you safe."

They sat in their chairs, drinking and eating, as the red sun dropped toward the water. "Why don't we go fix a light supper?" Charley said. They'd eaten the chips and drank the drinks. "I know what you're thinking, but we can eat on the patio. We won't miss the sunset."

Together they peeled and deveined the shrimp. Evie boiled the pasta and made a green salad. Charley cooked the shrimp on the grill and wiped off the table and chairs on the patio. Evie set the table and Charley uncorked a bottle of chardonnay.

When the food was served, they faced the Gulf. By then the sun was hovering over the water. It sunk out of sight rather quickly, and Charley lit the tiki torches around the screened-in lanai.

Evie was fading fast. A vodka and tonic and a couple glasses of wine were finishing her off, but she wasn't ready for bed. She didn't want this day to end.

Charley watched her with concern. "It's been a long day. I'm tired, aren't you?"

She helped Evie out of her chair and followed her to the bedroom. There, she pulled Evie's sweatshirt over her head. Gently, she slid the straps down Evie's arms and eased the swimsuit off, kneeling as she did so. After kissing Evie's cooling body, she helped her onto the sheets and covered her.

As she walked away, Evie reached for her but missed. "Where you going?" Evie asked, her eyes closing, her mind losing its battle to stay awake.

CHAPTER THIRTEEN

A week passed. Every day was hot and sunny with a cooling breeze off the Gulf. Evie thought she could live like this forever—making love in the cool of the morning, walking the beach in search of shells, chasing each other into the water, reading, and eating lunch. Making love in the afternoon. Back to the beach to read and swim some more. Drinks and appetizers on the beach, fixing dinner together, opening a bottle of wine and dining on the patio while the sun fell into the sea.

When the phone rang, Evie jumped. She had grown unaccustomed to such noises. Here they heard birds and screeching seagulls, speedboats and yachts, the waves meeting the beach, the sound of their own voices, and occasional comments from the men who patrolled the island's waters. At night these men would make fires on the sand. At first Evie wanted to join them or at least take them something to eat or drink, but Charley said they never became friendly with these men. It interfered with their jobs.

"How?" Evie asked.

"They begin to think they're part of the family. They lose sight of what they're supposed to be doing and become more like those guys who wanted to beach here. Remember them?"

She did. They had to be chased away every day for a week, which was probably when their vacation ended. She was looking at the trees that grew in every direction around the bungalow. "Are there poisonous snakes here?"

Charley looked at her, a slight frown wrinkling her forehead. "I don't know. Are you going for a walk?"

"Want to go with me?"

"I have to return my dad's call."

Evie looked for snakes as she walked. There were lots of geckos and salamanders on the ground and in the trees. They would make good snake food. They were in the house too, climbing the walls. She came across a giant toad and watched it lumber off into the sparse undergrowth. She recognized a few trees and other flora. She saw palmettos growing, but they were more of a bush than a tree. Palm trees were part of the forest, but she couldn't differentiate one from the other. When there was an opening in the trees, she stopped dead at the sight of the Caribbean spread out in all directions. Its vast expanse and varying colors filled her with awe. Boats dotted its surface. Was it the Caribbean Sea or the Gulf of Mexico? She'd have to ask.

She sneezed and reached for a tissue in the pockets of the old shorts she had put on that morning. She pulled out a crumpled piece of paper along with two dusty tissues and blew her nose. Smoothing out the paper, she stared at the words written in big and bold letters. Ted's writing, she thought, looking around fearfully. Could someone be hiding in the woods? She stuffed the note and tissues back in her pocket and began walking again.

Was this what everyone was looking for: Ballmount 117? She figured it was a lockbox in a bank somewhere. Eventually, she walked out of the woods and onto the beach. She didn't know which way was faster, left or right, so she turned the way her instinct told her to go—to the right. She saw their protectors or guards out in the boat, watching her. She wondered what they knew about why she and Charley were here. Something told her to keep going at the same pace, so she did. It seemed to take forever to get back to where she and Charley had been sitting.

Charley looked up at her from under the brim of her sun hat, her eyes mirroring the water. "Have a nice hike?"

"How big is this island?"

"Five miles long, two miles wide. Why?"

"I saw this huge toad. It was as big as my hand."

"A cane toad. They are huge and they'll eat anything. Don't pick them up, though. They've got poisonous glands."

Evie looked out at the water. The boat was offshore now, like it was following her. The two men's heads turned toward them. She sat down in her chair and picked up her Kindle, thinking about when she would tell Charley. She didn't want to spoil the rest of the day. She loved making love after lunch, their walks on the shore, the drinks and snacks on the beach, and dinner on the patio as the sun dropped into the water.

"What did you talk to your dad about?"

"Someone broke into your house last week. They didn't catch him."

She put her hand on her pocket but said nothing. "I'm glad I'm not there."

"Ready for lunch?" Lunch was always light, a half-sandwich and a piece of fruit.

"Sure," she said. "Want me to get it?"

"Nope. You can do it tomorrow."

While Charley was upstairs, Evie removed the note from her shorts and put it among the pages in Charley's book. After lunch, they walked the beach, picking up shells to add to their growing collection. They went after the same shell, a perfect conch, and fell into a fit of giggles. Evie came up with the shell.

"You are filthy," Charley said, laughing.

"And you think you aren't?" Evie asked and Charley chased her into the water.

Evie rolled over under the waves and found her footing. She still had the shell. And Charley chased her to shore. Laughing, they walked to their chairs.

As the sun began its descent toward the sea, Charley asked, "Ready for drinks and snacks?"

"Always. I'll get them," Evie offered.

"No need for both of us to go. I'll be back in no time."

Evie lay back in the chair. She felt gritty. Her hair was full of sand. A shower after supper would feel good. Right now, though, she was so sleepy. Her eyes closed of their own volition. She felt her mouth open, but she couldn't shut it.

She came-to rather sluggishly. She was being jostled. Confused, she wondered why Charley was pulling her arms. She started to tell her to stop it, but something was stuffed in her mouth. Her eyes popped open and she realized it wasn't Charley who was pulling her to her feet. Two men dragged her toward a boat on the beach. She tried to spit out what was in her mouth, but the men passed her to a third guy, who forced her onto the floor of the boat and tied her to the anchor rope. She struggled to get away but found she couldn't move. One of the men pushed the boat into the water and jumped in as someone else started the motor. By the time she spit the bandanna out of her mouth, the boat was speeding out to sea. Her screams were drowned out by the sound of the motor.

She managed to sit up and was horrified by how quickly the scenery had changed. She was only glad that she'd put the note in the pages of Charley's book. However, she knew something now, something they could force out of her. How good an actress was she? Just before she hit the floor, she'd seen Charley running from the house.

When the boat finally slowed and drove onto shore, the sun was hovering above the horizon. The man who had tied her to the anchor rope, untied her and dragged her across the beach to a small cottage on the other side of a dune.

Wet and covered with sand, she shivered in the cooling air. The men laughed and talked together in Spanish as they turned on an overhead light and tied her to a wooden chair. Then they left. She heard the boat's motor start up and grow fainter as it drove away.

Evie was hungry and she had to pee. She wriggled on the chair, trying to hold her urine. A leg on the chair gave way and it fell, taking her with it. She untangled her legs from the rope and banged back and forth, trying to break the back of the chair. She was making so much noise, she failed to hear a door open.

When she suddenly couldn't move, she looked up. A man was standing behind her, his foot on the back of the chair. Pot-bellied and greasy-haired, he looked ageless to her. She stared up at him and peed on the seat of the chair. It was such a relief, she shut her eyes and tried to ignore the unpleasant smell and warm wetness.

The man pulled a jackknife out of his back pocket and snapped it open, and her heart stopped. Leaning over her, he cut the ropes and jerked her to her feet. "That was disgusting. Don't you know how to hold your water, little lady?" He looked her over. "You're filthy." He led her to a door and flung it open. "Take a shower before the boss gets here." He pushed her into the room and shut the door.

She felt along the wall and flipped a switch. An overhead light came on and she took in the rectangular box of a room. In one corner was a metal shower with rusty interior walls and a curtain. Along one wall was a toilet and a rusty sink. Over it was a mirror so old and scratched, she could hardly see herself. Next to the shower was a shabby towel on a rack. There was no window, no way out and no lock on the door. She turned the water on and stepped under it. She used shampoo from a bottle in a corner of the stall and a skinny bar of soap in a rusted rack under the showerhead to soap her body and swimsuit, then rinsed off. She figured it was the quickest shower she'd ever taken. And the first one wearing a swimsuit.

In the metal cabinet above the sink she found another shabby towel, but at least it was clean. Underneath it was an ancient dryer. She dried off as best she could and used the dryer to dry her suit and hair.

Someone banged on the door. "Time's up. Come on out." It was the voice of the man who had untied her.

She ran her fingers through her hair, wrapped the towel around her swimsuit and opened the door.

PART II

CHAPTER FOURTEEN

Charley dropped the tray and ran inside for the key to the boat. She had been at the top of the hill when Evie was pushed to the floor of the boat as it backed away and sped off into deeper water before turning and following the shore. She ran to the dock, wondering where the men were who were supposed to keep their island safe.

She jumped into the MasterCraft, dropped the key, picked it up and jammed it in place. The starter didn't crank; nothing happened. She opened the engine cover, saw the wires dangling from the battery and wrenched them in place. When the engine roared in response, she slipped the lines off the posts and backed out. Speeding toward a boat that seemed to be keeping the same pace, never getting any closer or any further away, seemed hopeless. But she couldn't stop, even though she didn't know if Evie was in the boat she was following.

Fumbling for her phone, she called her brother Jeremy, shouting into the receiver.

"They took her, Jer. When I went up to the house, they came ashore and grabbed Evie. I saw one of them push her to the bottom of their boat as they fled."

"What's all that noise? Are you chasing them?" he shouted back.

"I have to," she yelled.

"And what are you going to do if you catch them?" He sounded angry.

"I've got a gun."

"That's a good way to get killed. Turn back, Charley. I'll get Tony and we'll be there in a few hours."

"I have to see where they take her." She was getting hoarse.

"Don't do anything else. Come back to the island. We're on our way."

"I think we have a problem with these guys who are supposed to keep people off the island."

"Seems that way. See you soon. Don't get yourself killed, Charley. That won't help anyone."

The craft was bouncing on incoming waves. She had kept her eye on the retreating boat through the conversation with Jeremy, and now the boat was gone. She idled her craft and ran down into the cabin where she grabbed one of her brother's sweatshirts and pulled it on. From a peg she took a cap that belonged to her dad. She stuffed her hair under it and pulled the brim low.

When she got on deck again, the MasterCraft was drifting toward shore. Cruising slowly a few hundred feet offshore, she scanned the beach for the boat that had taken Evie. The sweatshirt hung below her hips. She hoped she looked like any fisherman returning home.

When she saw the men pushing a boat into the water and jumping in it, she felt the blood pulse quickly through her veins. Certain that these men were Evie's kidnappers, she looked for Evie. The boat with the men sped into deep water, passing her bow by maybe a hundred feet. She almost missed seeing the neglected cottage set back behind the dune, and dropped a marker off the far side of the boat. It floated on the surface, invisible to the unknowing eye. The rundown cottage was flanked on either side by condominiums.

She idled close to one of the condos, turned off the engine and dropped the anchor. She put a foot on the step next to the transom and lowered herself into the water. By now it was completely dark, but the windows in the little shack were dimly lit. She peeked in a window. A man was sitting at a table, smoking a cigarette, looking straight at her. Heart pounding, she froze in place before realizing he couldn't see her in the dark as long as she stood still. When he looked away, she moved to another window. She crept around the cottage. There were two tiny bedrooms and a kitchen with a greasy stove, an old fridge and a rusty sink. She was in the shadows when a car pulled into the sandy yard and a man got out. He was tall and wore khaki pants and a polo shirt. His bald head glowed in the light over the back door. There was no sign of Evie.

She went back to her craft and backed into deeper water before idling away, studying the places along the shore, forming a mental image of where she was. When she thought she was far enough away, she throttled up, turned on the lights and headed toward her island.

She tied the lines, leaped to the dock and grabbed Evie's Kindle and her book on her way to the stairs. After taking the steps two at a time, she hurried inside. No one was there. She looked at her phone and saw a text from Jeremy. *Come and get us. We're at the dock.*

Her brothers were waiting, dressed in long, baggy shorts, their feet dangling over the edge of the pier. They tossed their bags in the boat and climbed aboard.

"How did you get here so fast?" she asked.

"We were already on our way," Tony said as he stood next to her.

"I have to show you where they took Evie. We have to go now." She steered to the cottage between the condominiums and dropped anchor.

They all climbed out of the boat and approached the cottage. People were sitting at the dock next door, talking and drinking. Tony waved and someone waved back.

"I could use a drink right now," Jeremy said quietly. He was carrying a handgun.

The rundown cottage was dark. Tony tried the door and it opened. They walked inside and Tony turned on a flashlight. A broken chair lay on the floor. Jeremy turned on the overhead light and Charley blinked. She crossed the room to an open door and flipped on the light. It was the bathroom, and it was apparent that the shower had been used recently. Something sparkled on the floor and she bent down and picked up one of Evie's earrings. She cursed herself, realizing Evie must have been in the bathroom when she looked in the windows.

"I found her earring in there," she told her brothers.

They searched the place thoroughly and came up with nothing else.

"Let's go," Jeremy said. "We have to call the police. That earring will have her DNA on it. I'll keep it dry." He took it from Charley, who was still in her swimsuit with the sweatshirt over it. She'd taken off the ballcap, and her blond hair hung disheveled on her shoulders.

She was terrified for Evie. What were they doing to her? She sat, cold and numb in the back of the boat as it sped toward the island.

"Where are those guys who are supposed to keep people off the island?" Tony said angrily when they docked the boat. "I didn't see them when we got here the first time or when we left, and I don't see them now."

Charley picked up on his words. "They were part of it, I bet. They never would have let the boat that took her away land on the island."

"You're right," Jeremy said. "I wonder what happened to the guys we hired. I'll call that firm tomorrow."

They went upstairs to the bungalow. Jeremy was going to call the police, so Charley went into the bedroom to change. She stripped off her swimsuit and put on sweats. Evie's shorts were lying half off a chair where Charley had dropped them. She picked them up and buried her face in them, smelling suntan lotion, then put them on the chair.

When she went looking for her brothers, Tony was in the kitchen. "Want a sandwich, Charley?"

"Where is Jeremy?" she asked.

"Looking for the guys who were supposed to be guarding the beach."

"Don't you think you should be with him? They might be dangerous."

"You're right. He's got a gun, though."

"They might have guns, too."

"Someone has to stay with you." He took a huge bite and chewed. "I don't know where he is anyway."

Charley picked up her book. She'd never be able to concentrate now. Her bookmark fell to the floor, and she bent to pick it up. She put it between two pages, and a scrap of paper floated to the floor. She grabbed it and saw the writing: Ballmount 117. It was a new book. There hadn't been anything in it but her bookmark.

She stuffed the paper in her pocket. What if…she thought. She felt a tap on her shoulder and went ballistic.

"Hey, it's just me," Tony said. "I'm sorry about your girlfriend. I hadn't eaten all day."

She stared at him. "I'm going to lie down. Lock the door if you go out."

She found five Ballmount Banks in Tampa. Four were branches. She wanted to call her dad and ask his advice. Evie was her client and Charley was in over her head. They still hadn't changed attorneys. She was looking at the website, wondering what she should tell the police, when her two brothers came in the door. She heard their voices in the other room, along with another she didn't recognize.

Jeremy knocked on her door. "You need to come out, Charley."

"Coming." She got up and looked in the mirror. She didn't want to look like a crazy person, so she brushed her hair before joining her brothers.

Two police officers, a man and woman, were sitting on the edge of their chairs. Her brothers were on the couch. Jeremy introduced the two as Officer Cynthia Pellman, an attractive African American woman, and Officer James Babcock, who looked like he should still be in high school. He even had zits.

Charley sat on the desk chair and told them she was Evie's attorney, that she had brought her here to keep her safe until the men who kept breaking into her house after her husband's murder were found and arrested. Evie had been accosted by one of these men.

"She was kidnapped off your beach by a number of men?" Cynthia asked.

"Yes, but not the ones who broke into her house. That was in Wisconsin. I followed their boat to this little cottage set back off the water between two condominium complexes and saw the men leave in the boat without Evie. It was dark, a light was on in the cottage, but I didn't see her inside. I saw a man, and after I looked in all the windows, another man drove in. Neither saw me."

Pellman asked, "How can you be sure the men who kidnapped her were not connected to the ones who broke in the house?"

"I can't, of course," Charley said.

"And why were men breaking into her house?" Pellman asked.

"They were looking for something her husband must have hidden before he was killed. Something valuable. Anyway, I went to get my brothers. We returned to the cottage, but no one was there."

She had told her brothers not to say nothing about the earring, not yet. Her brother had given it to her for safekeeping. They were architects. She was the attorney. She thought that was why they kept quiet.

Jeremy said, "We hired a firm to send two men to patrol the waters around the island. Otherwise, people come onshore and party."

"They didn't stop this boat from landing or try to protect the woman?" Pellman asked.

"No. And when we got back from looking for Evie, they were gone."

"We're thinking these guys are working for someone else besides the firm we hired," Tony put in.

"Certainly sounds like it."

"I know the cottage you're talking about. We'll check it out," Officer Babcock put in.

"Tonight? Tomorrow? Time is crucial," Charley said.

"As soon as we leave," Pellman promised. "I'll call you after we've been there." She looked from one to another. She was young, maybe thirty-five at the oldest. Eager.

"Can I go with you?" Charley asked.

"No. Sorry. It's against department rules. We'll find the cottage."

Charley and Pellman exchanged cards and the officers left.

"Do you want something to eat now?" Tony asked her.

"Thanks, but no. I have to make a call."

"I'll make supper and you have to eat, Charley. I mean it."

Jeremy looked skeptical. "Who can you call this time of night?"

"Dad. I've got questions for him."

In her room, she put in her dad's number. "Hey, Dad," she said when he picked up.

"Your brothers told me your girlfriend was kidnapped. Are they with you? Have you found her?"

"No, Dad. You remember the Harrington case, right? Men kept breaking into the house, trying to find whatever her murdered husband had hidden. Has anyone found out anything more about this case? You said her house was broken into again." She told her father that the men hired to protect the island were apparently crooked.

"Well, get rid of them. I'm sorry, honey. I have to get ready for some event I'm going to with your mom. If I learn anything more, I'll call you."

Tony was pounding on her door. "Come eat," he yelled.

CHAPTER FIFTEEN

Officer Pellman called around nine thirty. "Is this Ms. Webster?"

"Officer Pellman? Call me Charley."

"Call me Pellman. We went to the cottage. No one there. Searched it thoroughly. Took fingerprints. Now we're trying to match them. Do you have anything with your friend's fingerprints?"

"Yes. Her Kindle. My book."

"We'll swing by tomorrow morning and take her Kindle. Okay?"

"Yes, of course."

As soon as she hung up, she realized she hadn't asked exactly what time when they were going to "swing by." She went into the main room, where her brothers were watching TV. They both looked at her.

"How was Dad?" Jeremy asked.

"The same. That was Officer Pellman on the phone. She and Officer Babcock are coming by tomorrow for Evie's Kindle.

They need something with fingerprints on it to compare against the fingerprints they lifted in the cottage. I'm going to lie down."

"First you should eat something," Tony said.

"Okay."

She knew she wouldn't sleep. She was still looking at the ceiling long after the bungalow went quiet. Midnight, according to her watch. She heard noises, voices. Someone was partying on the beach. She pulled on shorts, locked her windows and bedroom door, crept through the living room. Someone was there in the dark. She pointed her gun. "Stop right there or I'll shoot you."

"That's how people kill family," Tony said.

Horrified, she dropped her arm. "Sorry. I heard voices."

"Yeah, me too." Jeremy joined them.

They went outside, locked the door and spread out, six feet apart. From the hilltop, in the moonlight, Charley saw the empty boat on the beach. She figured kids were using the beach for partying. "Why don't you two hike the perimeter. I'll stay here."

Her brothers went in opposing directions, following the path the three of them had made in childhood.

She sat on a stump near the top of the steps to the beach, struggling to stay awake. After almost falling off the stump several times, she wished she had chosen to walk around the island.

The water lapped against the shore. No wind tonight. The sound was hypnotic. Far out, a ship was lit up against the darkness. She watched the beach until her eyes no longer registered it. She thought of Evie, reliving their time together, but even that wasn't keeping her awake. The sound of shots made her jump.

Below her, four men were scrambling to get in the boat. She ran down the stairs, stumbling twice. Her legs were cramping from sitting so long. She rushed toward the vessel, which was a hollowed-out boat with four seats and a 75 HP motor, the same one that had taken Evie away. She pointed her handgun at the guy pushing off. These men were the ones who had taken Evie.

"I'll shoot if you don't put your hands up. The man pushing the boat away from shore continued to do so, and she shot him in the buttocks. He cursed and fell to the beach, clutching his rear end. Another man took an oar and began pushing off. She shot him in the hand. He dropped the oar and screamed. Two more men, who were running toward the boat, turned and ran the other way. They were stopped by Tony, who shot one in the foot. The men in the boat scrambled out and put their hands up.

Jeremy walked down the steps, phone in hand. "I called Officer Babcock. He and his partner, the lady officer, and backup are on their way."

The uninjured men jumped into the boat, started the motor and began backing out as Tony and Jeremy shot holes in the boat. It began to sink, and Tony waded out to grab it and pull it in. The men jumped out and ran down the beach, calling to each other in Spanish.

Tony and Jeremy ran up the hill toward the other side of the island. "You'll be all right?" Tony asked Charley before he left.

"Take your shirts off and tie them tight above the wound to stop the bleeding," Charley ordered the men on the beach.

"Can you help?" the man she'd shot in the hand asked.

"Let one of your friends help."

She saw the knife in the hand of the man with the wounded foot before he threw it. The knife came spinning toward her with remarkable speed and accuracy. It pierced the connecting tissue between her arm and body. She still held the gun on them, but it was wavering and so was she. She pulled the trigger. The shot echoed in her ears as her legs caved.

Voices faded. She whimpered and came to when the knife was pulled out. Jeremy was wrapping her armpit and the shoulder that Tony was holding. They put her in their boat. "Wha…Who…" she tried to ask.

"The police are taking over," Tony said. "Pretty hot shooting, Char."

That last shot. Where had it gone? "Did I kill…"

"No. Your shot alerted us and we came running. One of those guys was going for your gun. No one's dead. Remember those are rubber bullets."

She closed her eyes and gave herself over to the place between being aware and unaware. Her brothers put her in the cruiser. Tony held the tourniquet, made from one of their T-shirts, tight between her heart and the wound. The sound of the motor penetrated her consciousness. She opened her eyes and looked at the dark sky lit by stars and wondered if she was imagining it.

On shore, her body was moved from hands to hands and onto a gurney. Shoved into the ambulance, she rocked back and forth as the siren screamed, struggling not to fall off. When she opened her eyes, everything was white. Again, she was jostled.

Someone said, "One, two, three…" And the next time she opened her eyes, she was in a bed with tubes running to her body.

Her brothers stood next to the bed, smiling. "Hey, Char," Jeremy said, and she closed her eyes. They didn't look like twins. Both were tall, but Jeremy was broad in the shoulders and chest, and his hair and eyes were the color of dark chocolate. Tony was lanky, with sandy-colored hair and eyes like milk chocolate. But they were alike in all other ways—the way they walked, their gestures, the inflections of their voices, their laughs.

"She's smiling," she heard Tony say.

"Wonder what she's thinking," his brother said. Their voices made her feel safe, and she fell asleep.

Before she left the hospital the next day, the doctor gave her a script to fill and told her to rest and come back in a week, so he could check the wound, sooner if there was unusual bleeding. "Eat lots of protein. It helps with healing."

She nodded and thanked him. Her shoulder and the connecting tissue were wrapped with one bandage that spread across her upper chest. Her arm hung in a sling. Fortunately, it was her left arm. The doctor had said it would take physical therapy to help restore its use.

She rode back to the dock with her brothers. It hurt terribly whenever the car hit a bump or a break in the pavement. She shut her eyes and gritted her teeth. She wasn't looking forward to the boat ride to the island or to climbing the steps.

Officers Pellman and Babcock met them at the dock. After Charley climbed carefully out of the car, they told her they had identified the men in the little cottage through their fingerprints. An alert was out to find them. The men who had kidnapped Evie were in jail, charged with kidnapping. The ones who had been shot were in the hospital under armed guard.

Tony helped her into the cabin cruiser. She bit her lip, trying not to cry out. She thought she was a sissy and then felt terrible because Evie might be suffering far worse.

"Go slow," she said as Jeremy got behind the wheel.

At the island, her brothers helped her onto the dock and up the stairs to the bungalow.

She let out a sigh once she'd carefully lowered herself onto the bed. Her brothers stood, looking at her, shuffling their feet.

"Sorry it hurts so much," Jeremy said.

"I hope it's better tomorrow. Are you asleep, Charley?" Tony asked.

"No. Better not call Mom. She'll come and take care of me."

"Is that so bad?" Tony asked.

"She will insist I stay in bed, and I can't. Please don't say anything to her or Dad yet."

"Okay. Unless you don't eat."

"C'mon, Tony. I'm not hungry." Tony was always hungry.

"Protein, the doctor said."

She was drifting away on a dream.

The next day she was on her feet. Jeremy had called the firm and was given many apologies and offers of a refund. Two new men appeared to take the places of the two who had disappeared. These were young, friendly guys, who often beached their boat to talk. But it was awfully hard to believe they too hadn't been bought.

Jeremy told Charley that their mother was coming to stay with her. He and Tony had to go back to work.

"I asked you not to tell Mom and Dad. You went behind my back."

"We can't leave you here alone."

"Like Mom is going to keep us safe."

She loved her mother, who was smart and pretty but small in stature. She and her brothers got their height from their father. Her dad called her mother his *Little Woman*. Charley thought that was patronizing and wondered why her mother only laughed.

"She's a deadly shooter. Better than you. Better than me and Tony and Dad. She hates guns, but when she shoots one, she never misses. She's the reason we have rubber bullets."

"How do you know that?" Charley was intrigued. Her mom forbade weapons in the house. She'd never seen her pick up a gun. Her dad hid his handgun in a boot in the bedroom closet.

"When we were teasing her about not being able to hit a wall, she took my handgun and emptied the ammo into a bullseye."

"She went to a shooting range?"

"We were target shooting in their backyard," Tony said with a laugh. "We thought she was grocery shopping. You know what Mom looks like when she's mad."

"Yeah, I do. Like an angry wren, but she'll ditch my handgun."

"Not when she sees your wound."

The men patrolling their shores took her brothers to the dock. Charley went down to the beach, feeling useless. Unable to concentrate on anything, and obsessing about Evie, she stared at the sea until her eyes registered nothing. When the boat came toward her shore, though, she focused on the three people in it. It was at that moment she realized how vulnerable she was.

The boat docked across from the cabin cruiser. One man got out and helped her mother onto the dock. She wore jeans and a short sleeve pullover with a V-neck. The other man put a suitcase on the dock, which the first man picked up. The two guys were the ones guarding the island's shores.

"How the hell did she get here so fast?" Charley said aloud as she rose to her feet.

Her mother's hand was tucked into one young man's elbow, while he hefted the suitcase with his other arm. His muscles popped out from his T-shirt, which had the name of the firm, *Protection Inc.*, and under it, *Matt*.

"Hello, sweetheart," Charley's mother said, staring at all the bandaging. "I better not hug you. Let's get my suitcase inside and talk."

Matt followed them to the bungalow and set the suitcase next to the door.

"Thank you, Matt. You've been so helpful." She held out two five-dollar bills.

"Oh no," he said. "We're not allowed to accept tips, but thank you."

"Thank you," she said, turning to Charley.

"Can we talk on the patio?" Charley asked.

"Sure." They watched Matt jog down the steps to the boat. "He seems like a nice young man. I always forget how beautiful it is here."

Charley sat down carefully on one of the straight chairs around the table.

"Hurts like hell, I suppose."

"It'll get better."

"Is it hard to breathe?"

"It's not hard. It just hurts. I'm sorry you thought you had to come."

"I wanted to come. I would have come right away had I known. Now tell me the story about this woman who was kidnapped."

Charley told her the story, leaving out her love affair with Evie. Her mother, whose name was Reenie, a nickname for Maureen, had placed a hand on her chest while listening.

"We have to rescue her," Reenie said.

"How, Mom? We don't know where she is."

"Then we'll find out." Reenie stood and paced.

"How do we do that? The police don't know where she is."

"Do they know who took her?"

"They identified them from their fingerprints."

"What are their names?"

"I wrote them down. They're on the desk."

"I'll get them." Her mother went into the house and came out with a notepad. "Calvin Rafferty and Pat Wingate? Otherwise known as Rafe and the Gator."

"If that's what it says." Her wound ached.

"Let me get my computer out." She went inside and emerged with her Mac, which she opened on the table. She glanced at Charley. "Why don't you go lie down, darling? This might take a while."

She didn't believe her mother would find the men, of course. "I think I will. Wake me if you find out anything at all." She went inside and placed herself carefully on her bed and closed her eyes.

When her mother sat on the bed, she awoke with a gasp. Her eyes flew to the clock on the dresser. She'd been asleep almost two hours. She could hardly believe it. She tried to sit up but couldn't. Her left arm was useless. The wound and her shoulder were screaming. She wanted to scream too, but instead said, "What, Mom?"

"I found Gator."

"Where? How? Did you call Officers Pellman and Babcock?"

"Not yet. I thought I would go over and see if I could find out more about him."

"What? And get yourself kidnapped too?"

"Maybe I'll find Evie."

"No, Mom. I have only one mother and I'm not going lose her in some brainless scheme." Again, she tried to sit up and fell back, panting. This time she yelped.

Her mother put a gentle hand behind her back and helped her sit with her feet on the floor. "I could find out what kind of car he drives, get the license plate number and other useful things."

"Can't the police find those things out from the DMV?"

"Let's have dinner and talk about it."

"I'm not hungry."

"You need to eat protein to heal. I've fixed a chicken salad, which we can eat on the lanai or inside. Which would you like?"

She thought she wanted to eat outside, but once out there, she was so uncomfortable, she wanted to go inside, where she was just as uncomfortable.

Feeling as if she had been reduced to a little girl made her grumpy, which led her to think she was behaving like one. The salad was good, and she remembered the doctor telling her to eat protein. So, she did.

After dinner, she went to bed but began to think about Evie and couldn't sleep. She heard her mother talking on the phone. She rolled to the edge of the bed and stood. She brushed her teeth and hair. Her hair had a little wave and curled on her shoulders. No way could she tie it back.

She popped a pain pill and went out onto the lanai, where her mother had a wine glass in one hand and was pressing her phone to her ear with the other. "We don't want to scare him away," she said.

Charley sat down and poured a glass of wine. She was sipping it, watching the blurry lights of fishing boats. The stars overhead blurred too. They floated on the water with the moon, rippling with the gentle waves. She thought she saw Evie coming up the stairs and stood to say something to her, but then she sat down and fell asleep.

CHAPTER SIXTEEN

She awoke in her bed and tested the wound by moving her shoulder. The pain was nothing she couldn't handle. In the bathroom, she washed her face and body as well as she could with one hand. Her hair hung lank. God, this was so inconvenient.

The bottle of tramadol was not on the sink where she had left it. She looked in the cabinet. Nothing but Tylenol and Tums. She struggled to pull on shorts and went to the kitchen, where her mother was frying eggs.

For a moment, she saw her mother as a person. Her sandy bob curled just below her ears. Her skin, usually pale, was slightly burned by the sun. Dressed in shorts and a short-sleeve pullover, her body curved in all the right places. Charley hoped she'd look as good at sixty-five. Her mom turned piercing blue eyes on her, reminding her that her small, nicely put-together mother was someone to be reckoned with.

"My hair needs washing, Mom."

"After breakfast. Come sit down."

"Where's my tramadol?"

"I have it. You're too big for me to carry."

"I'm sorry. I took too many, I think. I won't do it again. I didn't like the way I felt."

Her mother put a plate of refried beans, two fried eggs, and toast in front of Charley along with the bottle of tramadol, then sat down with her own.

"Want to go for a ride after we wash your hair?"

"Where?"

"To the Gator's."

Fear swamped her. "These people are dangerous. I've got this wound to prove it."

"That's exactly why we have to find your girlfriend. We're not going to confront him. We're going to follow him."

She stared at her mother until she returned the look. "You want to find your girlfriend, don't you?"

"You aren't very big and I'm not much use right now. I'm afraid one of us might get killed."

So, why were they driving around the city looking for Hayward Street? Her mother was behind the wheel of an old Ford Focus, which she had rented. She'd told Charley they wanted to be inconspicuous. Charley had found Hayward Street on her smartphone and was giving directions.

Charley had choked down her food and now she was glad she'd hardly eaten. She was sure she would puke otherwise.

Hayward Street where she thought the Gator resided looked abandoned. Sheets hung in the windows and paint was peeling off the siding. The yard had bare patches in the too-long grass. They parked up the street a block and waited.

Just when Charley was sure that nobody was at the house, a black Nissan shot out of the dirt driveway and toward the cross street. Her mother turned the key and the chase was on. They were half a block behind the sedan when it turned onto the interstate. Her mother stepped on the gas and followed.

When the Nissan passed a vehicle, her mom did the same. She kept her eye on the car with amazing accuracy. The two cars exited and headed for the Gulf. They followed the road that paralleled the water, zipping past the few cars on the road, always managing to keep a little more than a block between their car and the Nissan.

Charley was terrified. She clung to the door handle. "Did you ever drive a race car, Mom?"

"Not funny, Char."

"Dad's going to kill me if he finds out about this."

"He won't. And you do not control me, nor does he."

"Just so he knows that."

She was talking because she was nervous.

When the sedan turned into the narrow sandy drive to the little cottage, they sped past and turned into the condo driveway and parked in the guest parking area. Thick bushes with brilliant red bougainvillea flowers separated them from the little rundown cottage. They found a gap in the foliage and watched as two men marched a woman out of the cottage.

"Get your gun out, Char, and call the officers."

"Evie," Charley murmured, momentarily paralyzed. Then she opened her door, stepped down, lifted her arm and aimed at the man's hand that was propelling Evie toward the car.

Two shots broke the silence, and Evie ran toward the sound of the weapons. Both men screamed and fell, grabbing the hands that had been targeted. The bald man got up, lifted a handgun with his other hand, and Reenie shot the hand. The man's gun fell to the ground and the other man aimed at them. Reenie shot that gun out of his hand. Charley pushed Evie into the back seat and slammed the door. She wasn't going to lose her again. Reenie started walking toward the fallen men.

"Wait, Mom. The cops are on the way. We have to hold them here."

The men were crawling toward the Nissan. Reenie shot holes in the tires. They paused and began crawling back to the cottage like newly hatched baby sea turtles scrambling toward the sea. Charley wondered who was in the cottage and what weapons were stashed inside.

She was putting more rubber bullets in her gun when she heard the approaching sirens. Four police cars drove into the cottage yard. Two more followed. She and her mother waited while the police surrounded the cottage and eventually dragged the men out.

Her mother climbed in behind the wheel and Charley slid in next to Evie, who was sitting straight up and staring at Charley. Charley tried to put her uninjured arm around her but couldn't.

Evie looked at Charley's bandage. "What happened?"

"Those guys who took you in their boat? One of them knifed me, but not before I wounded a few of them."

Evie's eyes were wide. "Why were they there?"

"I don't know. Do you?"

"Ted. Because of Ted," Evie said.

They sat in the car until the police came out with two men, whose hands were wrapped and their wrists handcuffed. They put them in different police cars. Pellman and Babcock walked up to the old Ford.

"You all right?" Cynthia asked.

Babcock nodded at Evie. "Can the lady come to the station and give a statement?"

Evie looked away. Charley couldn't tell what she was feeling. She seemed very distant.

"She's kind of traumatized," Reenie said.

"We can meet you on the island if that's all right," Evie said in a soft voice.

"We'll book these guys on kidnapping charges," Cynthia said. "And we'll come to the island. We can bring a recorder. That might be better all around. We have a few questions for you ladies." Pellman looked at Reenie, and Charley introduced her. "Maybe you can tell us why you were here."

"Thank you for putting them in jail," Reenie said.

They drove toward the island. Evie leaned into Charley's good shoulder. Her mother watched them in the rearview mirror but said nothing.

Back at the bungalow, Evie disappeared into the shower while Charley and her mom sat on the lanai. Charley looked at her mother with new eyes. She had always admired her father, and although she'd loved her mom, she had thought she was like most women married to wealthy, successful men—someone who managed the house and kids.

"Mom, when did you learn to shoot?"

Reenie sighed. "When my mother said I had to learn to protect myself. I don't know why she thought that, but she taught me how to shoot a jackpine cone off a stump."

"Grandma?" She was aghast.

"Yes. Your brothers taught you, I suppose."

"But I thought you didn't believe in the proliferation of guns."

"I don't. Most people who commit suicide shoot themselves with their own guns. Think of all the senseless deaths in this country caused by guns."

"Now by automatic weapons," Charley said. "Why didn't you work outside the home, Mom?"

"I did. I put your dad through law school. Once you kids were born, I stayed home. Why hire someone to take care of the children when you can do it yourself?"

"So, what are you doing now that we're grown up?"

"I'm writing."

Speechless with astonishment, she still managed to ask, "Writing what?"

Evie stepped out onto the lanai, wearing capris and a pullover with a V-neck. Charley wanted to devour her. She struggled to hide her lust from her mother. Besides, there was no way she could make love in her condition. She glanced at her watch.

"Do you want a little something to eat before the police get here?" Reenie asked. "I think we missed lunch."

Evie sat down next to Charley. "Don't go to any trouble for me," she said.

Reenie gave her a hard look and burst into laughter. "Honey, I think we already did. Food is easy."

Evie let out an embarrassed laugh and Charley glared at her mother. "I can help," Evie said. "Don't look at your mother like that, Charley. She's right."

"I made lunch this morning. You can help put some plates and forks on the table out here, Evie. Pretty name for a pretty woman."

Charley stayed put. She was useless carrying things. She stared at the water and wondered what their next move would be. Could they stay here and be safe? She hated the way she felt. This was the place she loved most and now it was tarnished.

Evie returned with the plates, forks and a knife to cut the bread and dropped a kiss on Charley's forehead. Charley smiled and reached for her hand, but Evie eluded her and went back into the bungalow. Evie and Reenie came back together, Evie with the glasses and Reenie with a bowl of chicken salad and a cutting board with a baguette and butter on it.

"Mmm. So good," Evie said, after a bite. "They fed me fast food. I don't think I'll ever eat it again."

Evie and Reenie had just finished cleaning up the dishes when the police officers climbed the steps. The two men who guarded the island had picked them up at the dock and would take them back. They met with Evie and Charley in the living room.

"So, what can you tell us about these men?"

Evie began to talk. She told them how she was taken to the small cottage and left there with a man called Gator. Rafe, the other man, had shown up later. She described the men and said she'd only known them by those names. She'd never seen them before. They had tied her hands and covered her eyes before driving her to a house, where they tied her hands and feet to a chair behind sheet-covered windows. During the day, she was tied to the chair, except when eating. At night, she was tied to a bed. They hadn't touched her inappropriately, and fed her whatever they were eating. One of them would take her to the bathroom and wait outside while she went. There was no window in the bathroom. "They said over and over that they'd let me go if I told them where my husband hid what they wanted. I would ask them what it was he'd hidden. We talked in circles."

"How did you happen to be at the cottage when we found you?"

"Gator took me there. He said he was going to turn me loose, but then Rafe showed up and the two of them began to argue about letting me go. They were taking me back to the house when Charley and Reenie rescued me. I saw them behind the bougainvillea." She smiled.

"And you don't know what your husband hid?" Babcock asked. "You don't have a clue?"

"No. He didn't tell me where he went or what he was doing. And since he was killed, men have been breaking into wherever I am staying and looking for something."

"Weren't the police involved after these break-ins?"

Charley had been holding her hand under the table and now squeezed it. Evie looked at her. "Yes. Police guarded my house for two days after Ted died but they couldn't do that forever. No matter where I moved, someone broke in during the night. I was knocked unconscious once and tied up at various times, but no one has tried to kill me. It's like a treasure hunt and I'm the only clue, but I'm clueless." She laughed a little. "It's no fun waking in the night, knowing someone is in the house."

Cynthia looked very serious. "Terrifying, I would think. It sounds like a ring of people, all looking for the same thing. What did your husband do for a living?"

"He worked for Brighton Papers in their marketing department. He traveled a lot. Toward the end, I wasn't sure he was working anymore, because he was gone so much. By then, he was emotionally abusive. Wouldn't tell me where he'd been or where he was going." Charley was squeezing her hand again.

"You're a witness, so you'll have to be here to testify."

"And when will that happen?" She hadn't seen her children or Rebecca in weeks.

Then Pellman changed tactics and turned to Charley. "Why were your mother and you at the cottage, shooting at those men,"

Charley's pulse jumped. "Looking for Evie."

"Why didn't you call us?"

"We did. It was just a little too late."

Pellman got up and went to the door. She asked Reenie to come in.

"I asked your daughter why you two went to the cottage without calling us?"

"Well, we were on that road and pulled into the condominiums when we saw some activity at the cottage. We called you, but you never would have gotten there in time. They were leading Evie out to the car."

"I see," Pellman said, her expression unreadable. "Well, stick around until Evie leaves. Okay?"

Her clever mom, Charley thought, fighting a smile.

When the police officers left, Evie asked Charley why she shouldn't let them know about Detective Jalinsky.

"I'll tell you later," she said.

CHAPTER SEVENTEEN

"It must have been horrific." Charley ran her fingers over the red, indented lines around Evie's wrists.

They were alone in Charley's bedroom. It was still hard for Evie to believe she was here. Even more difficult to believe how she got here.

"It was terrifying at first when I didn't know what they were going to do to me, but when all they did was ask the same questions over and over, it became numbingly boring. When you came along, I thought they were going to let me go." She looked into Charley's eyes, darkened by what she thought was desire, and smiled shyly.

Charley spoiled the mood by showing her the slip of paper with the name of the bank and a number, the one she had slipped into Charley's book just before she was kidnapped. "Do you know…"

Evie took the scrap of paper and dropped it on the books on the chair. "Not now."

She didn't want to think of the mindless hours spent tied to a chair or the first night, when she feared one or both men would come into the room and rape her. She was frantic for Charley to make love to her—to wash away what had happened with her hands and mouth. She reached for the hem of Charley's shirt.

Charley put her hand over Evie's, then gestured toward her wound. "This hurts like the knife is still in there."

"Who threw it?"

"One of the men who took you off the beach. They came back, maybe for me, maybe to look through the house." Charley leaned forward and kissed Evie.

God, Evie loved those kisses, the preview of what was to come. But it looked like she'd have to make the moves this time. She backed off a little and carefully removed Charley's shirt. She wore no bra. Evie lifted her breasts and kissed them tenderly.

Charley said, "Let's lie down." Her face was white, her lips pale.

"Are you up to this?" she asked, following Charley to the bed and watching her ever so carefully lower herself to the mattress.

Charley grimaced. "When have I ever not been up to this? But you'll have to make it happen." Charley had always been the initiator.

"You look awfully pale." Evie said, taking off Charley's shoes before pulling off her shorts and panties. She sat down and removed her own shoes and clothes and lay on her side and kissed the hurt shoulder.

She braced herself and made her way down Charley's body. When she reached the joining of Charley's legs, she hovered over Charley and spread her thighs. She heard Charley exhale as if she had been holding her breath. Immediately, she forgot everything except what she was doing.

"Put your leg over me," Charley whispered, and she pulled Evie down with her good arm when she complied.

After, Evie kissed Charley's wet face as she realized just how painful this act of love had been for Charley. "I'm sorry," she said, but she wasn't. She knew she would never forget the helplessness she'd felt when tied to a chair or bed. Such was her anger that Charley and her mother had not killed Rafe and Gator, she was consumed with it.

"Don't be," Charley said.

"Those men will post bail and be out of jail tomorrow."

"I don't think it will be that easy."

She brightened for a moment but said nothing.

"How did the note get in my book?" Charley asked.

Evie got up and retrieved the piece of paper from the chair. She read the ill-formed letters, as if written in haste. "How else? I found it in a pocket of that old pair of shorts I had on, where Ted must have put it, meaning to retrieve it, but then he was killed. Just before that boat landed and those guys took me, I slipped it in your book."

"Why don't we find out where that bank is and go there? That's probably a lockbox number."

"We can't. Someone would follow us. Besides, we don't have a key."

She had been curled against Charley's good shoulder and rolled away with a sigh. "I want this to be over. Let's give the note to the officers. They can get a court order to open the lockbox, if it is a lockbox."

"All right. We'll do it, but there's no way for my mother not to know."

"Why don't you tell her first and see what she says? She seems like a sensible woman."

"Char, do you know where this bank is?" Reenie asked. They were sitting in the lanai, drinking coffee the next morning.

"Yes. There are four branches in Tampa where the main building is."

Evie shot her a sharp look. Why hadn't Charley told her anything about the bank? At least, she assumed it was a bank.

Charley's mother asked, "Is this what I think it is? Is it stolen goods?"

"Probably," Charley said.

"Maybe you should call the officers."

Charley smiled at Evie. "Exactly what Evie said."

"Mrs…"

"Reenie. Call me Reenie."

"Mrs. Reenie…"

"Just Reenie."

"I'm tired of my home and Charley's being broken into, Reenie. I'm tired of being kidnapped and tied up. I feel terrible that I'm the reason Charley's wounded. We're going to give the note to the police officers. Maybe these crooks will leave us alone when the lockbox is emptied."

"Besides, Mom, if Evie and I, or you, managed to get our hands on what her husband was hiding, we might be charged with his murder."

Evie shivered as chills danced over her. She sipped her coffee and frowned at Charley. "But thank you, Reenie, for rescuing me from those men. I can never repay you or Charley."

Reenie gave Evie's arm a squeeze. "You're welcome. Reenie and Charley to the rescue." She laughed and they joined in.

"Don't. That hurts," Charley said, gasping.

After breakfast, Charley called Pellman and Babcock and asked if they could come over.

They were all sitting in the lanai. Reenie had made coffee for everyone. Charley gave the officers the piece of paper with the name of the bank and the lockbox number.

Evie told them how she had found it and who she thought had put it there.

"Give us a heads-up before we have to come back to testify," Charley said, giving Pellman her card. "We're going home."

"Until we've opened that box, which will probably take a judge's order, these guys will still be after Evie," Pellman warned.

Babcock said, "Watch your backs."

They were in the air in an hour. Reenie sat in the copilot's seat, next to Jeremy.

Evie watched the mother and son talking, their voices inaudible over the sounds of the engines. "Does your mother have a pilot's license?"

"Yes. So do I." Charley studied her a moment before smiling.

She squeezed Evie's arm. "Everything okay?"

"Yes," Evie said, thinking this family was definitely out of her league. The attraction must be just that. Financially, it could never lead to anything even remotely equal. But was money always the determining factor? She planned to take courses to renew her teacher's license.

"You're awfully quiet." Charley broke into her thoughts. "Are you worried about being home when I'm at work?"

"You know I've been thinking about teaching full-time. I'll have to renew my license, which means taking a few courses and a test. I'll probably do it online."

"You're brave, you know. After all that's happened."

"Not really. I put it out of my mind." Which wasn't true. She struggled to keep from thinking of it. "You and your mom are the brave ones."

"You must be looking forward to seeing Rebecca." Rebecca would be meeting them at the airport. "Want something to eat or drink?"

"I wouldn't pass up a cup of hot chocolate." She fell asleep after drinking it and only woke up when she felt as if she was falling out of the seat. The plane was tilting to the side, and she was startled to see the ground.

"Don't worry. Jeremy is turning. We're going to land at a field near Indianapolis and fill up."

Charley made sandwiches for all of them during the stop and passed them around before they took to the air again.

Evie thanked her and thought how strange the turn her life had taken when she met Charley. She had been raised in a lower middle-class family. They had lived in a three-bedroom Cape Cod. Her sister shared her room. The other bedroom her father used for an office. He was an insurance salesman. When her mom's father died, they came into an inheritance that allowed them to move to a larger house.

CHAPTER EIGHTEEN

Rebecca was waiting for them in the building near the hangar. She looked wonderful to Evie. The red highlights in her auburn hair shone in the light from a high window. She wore formfitting black slacks and a bright-blue cotton sweater.

Rebecca opened her arms and Evie walked into them. "Oh, how I missed you," Rebecca said.

"I missed you, too."

"What you texted me was hair-raising. The two men who were holding you captive are still behind bars, I hope. It's too awful to even think of."

"Charley and her mom shot the guns out of their hands and sent them crawling into the cottage where they'd taken me. They're quite the pair, the mother and daughter."

"And you caught the guys who kidnapped Evie, too?" she asked Charley, giving her a hug.

"My brothers and I managed that."

Evie said, "Here are three of the heroes. Charley, her mother, Reenie, and her brother Jeremy who flew us home.

Only her brother Tony is missing." She introduced Rebecca as her forever friend.

They shook hands and chatted for a few minutes. Jeremy asked Rebecca if she would take his mother home. He had to put the plane away.

"Of course," Rebecca said. "I'd be honored."

They wheeled the luggage out and stashed it in the trunk of Rebecca's Prius. Reenie sat up front with Rebecca. She told Rebecca she had a Prius, too and she loved it. Evie was surprised. She figured Reenie would have a Mercedes Coup. When they turned into a circular driveway with a two-story brick home and three-car garage set amidst a mature grove of trees, Evie was again surprised. She thought it modest compared to what she expected.

Rebecca took Reenie's suitcase out and wheeled it to the door. Charley and Evie followed with Reenie, who invited them all in for coffee or tea.

"Thanks Mom, for everything, but no, we need to get settled in."

Evie hugged Reenie and thanked her for saving her life.

Georgie met them at the door of the condo. Rebecca had taken him there before driving to the airport. Evie scooped him into her arms. Charley thanked Rebecca with a hug, and disappeared into her office.

"Thank God I didn't know you were kidnapped until you were rescued," Rebecca said once the two women were alone in the kitchen. "I still can hardly believe it. You had to be so scared."

Evie put the cat down and gave him a treat. "Well, they never hurt me. I thought maybe they were going to let me go when Charley and her mom showed up. At least, that's what one of them said. Hey, why don't I make some decaf? Can you stay a while?"

"No coffee, thanks. I can only stay a half hour or so."

"Tell me how my kids are and how it's going for you."

"Dave has been beside himself, calling and calling. You better call him."

"And Angie?"

"She has phoned. She doesn't understand why you went away without telling her."

"Hmm," she said. "What's happening with you?"

"I had lunch with Pam twice. She too is worried about you. I never really told anyone except John that you'd been kidnapped. I didn't exactly understand how it happened. It seemed so bizarre."

"I know. I kept telling myself this couldn't happen to me. I'd found a note that day with a bank's name and a number. It was in a pair of shorts that I took along. Ted must have put it in the pocket. When we left, we gave it to the two police officers down there who were assigned to my case."

"Do you think it's over now?" Rebecca's eyebrows arched in question.

"Maybe after word gets out that the lockbox is emptied if there's anything in it. God, I hope so. I'm so sick of being scared. Thank you for handling my kids. You are so much better at that than I am, especially Angie. I did email them when I got back to the island, but I wasn't there long. I'll call."

"Dave was so upset. He cried on the phone." She looked to where Charley had disappeared. "Tell me about Charley's family. They sound so interesting."

"They are. Reenie is against the proliferation of weapons, yet she can put a bullet exactly where she wants it to go. But they're rubber bullets. So can Charley, and no doubt her brothers can too. And they all have a pilot's license." She told Rebecca about the island and how Reenie seemed just like a regular mom most of the time. "It's like they live in another realm. One too rich for me."

"But you and Charley. You're an item now." It wasn't a question.

Evie shrugged. "I guess. Charley says we're just as boring as any other couple. But it isn't boring to me. It's still a novelty. I'm amazed when I think about what I'm doing, that this was hidden in me somewhere." She gazed at Rebecca as if she could give her an answer.

"Hey, it surprised me too."

"Angie will not be happy. I guess Dave came by it naturally, huh?"

When Rebecca left, unable to accept Evie's invitation to dinner, she said, "Send me an email after you talk to your kids, okay?" She hugged Evie again and kissed her on the cheek. "Don't go away for a long time," she said.

Charley was still in her home office so Evie called Dave.

"Mom? Where are you?"

Evie told him and they talked for a half hour. He said he was coming home the next day, so she told him she'd meet him there.

Next, she called her daughter. "Mom? Are you home?"

"I am."

And they talked for what seemed a long time. Angie sounded annoyed at first but mellowed after five minutes or so. She was going to her boyfriend's home on the weekend. Evie had thought of moving back to her house for a while after talking to Dave, but her conversation with Angie changed her thinking. She would call Dave and give him directions to Charley's.

He called when he left his apartment at nine the next morning. He said he should arrive around twelve thirty. But when one o'clock came and went and he hadn't shown up, Evie paced the floor. She had already washed the kitchen floor and bathrooms, vacuumed the hall and the bedroom Dave would sleep in. Then she vacuumed the other rooms and dusted every surface. She called his cell every half hour. The call went straight to voice mail. At four she called Charley, somewhat hysterical.

"Dave's not here. He's not answering his phone. He should have been here before one. Something is wrong." She knew she sounded frantic. She was frantic.

"Call the police. I'm on my way home."

She was punching in the number of the police department when her cell phone rang. She was so sure it was Dave, she answered it. "Hey. Where are you?"

"Your son is with us. He's safe, but how safe depends on you. You need to tell the next person who calls the information you've been hiding."

She was shocked into silence. The deep-voiced man hung up as the door to the garage opened. Her heart nearly exploded.

"What?" said Charley.

"They've taken Dave. I must give them the name of the bank and the number when someone calls back."

Charley stared at her. "Then that's what you'll do. After, we'll tell Pellman."

"No. We won't tell anyone until they release Dave."

"Okay," Charley said, before taking Evie in her arms. "Ask to talk to Dave before you tell them anything."

"How did you get home so fast?" Evie muttered into her good shoulder.

"I was halfway here when you called."

When the phone rang again, she nearly dropped it. Cautiously, she looked at the screen. Charley looked, too, and wrote down the numbers.

"Hello?" Evie said quietly. "Who is this?"

A man laughed. "It's Eddie, calling for the information."

"I want to talk to my son," she said, suddenly angry.

"He's safe."

"How do I know that?"

"Here. Talk to him."

"Mom?"

"Dave, are you all right?"

"I'm tied to a chair."

Just like they'd done to her. "Have they hurt you?"

"No. Mom, what's going on?"

Eddie, if that's who he was, said, "See? He's all right, and we'll release him when we get the information."

"I didn't know this information until recently," she said and gave him the name of the bank and the number.

"Soon as we find out whether there's anything to this info, we'll let him go."

"But you said…" The phone went dead.

Charley was talking on her phone and hung up when she heard Evie lash out with anger and fear. She pulled her close before asking what happened.

Evie sobbed, "We can't tell anyone until he's set free."

"They will let him go. They let you go." Her voice soothed Evie.

"No, they didn't. You and Reenie did." Evie's nose was crushed against Charley. She stopped crying and concentrated on breathing.

Charley's phone rang. She listened for a minute before saying, "I was afraid of that." She listened again. "I'll call you. We want to keep this quiet." She ended the call. "That was the police. The kidnapper's phone was one of those throwaway ones. He couldn't trace the number to anyone. Let's sit down and think about this."

Evie stared at her in disbelief. "My son is being held hostage and you want me to sit down."

"Yes, I do. We have to come up with a strategy. I'm thinking we have to talk to Pellman. She and Babcock are at risk now."

"But if there's anything in the lockbox, they probably have it by now. They should put back a large enough amount to satisfy these people."

Charley smiled. "Now you're thinking, honey."

"What if there was nothing there? It would be just like Ted to plant that note in my pocket, knowing there's nothing in the box."

"Do you want to call Pellman or Babcock?" Charley asked.

"Okay." She gave in. Maybe they could help. "Pellman has the brains. You know, though, the officers we talked to are going to tell Jalinsky. What are we going to say to Jalinsky?"

"We'll tell him the truth. What do you think?"

"I don't know." Her budding enthusiasm had collapsed. She slumped in a chair.

Charley made the call. She was talking to Pellman when the doorbell rang twice. Evie jumped and started to get up. Charley shook her head.

It rang again. Then Evie's cell registered a call. She looked at it as if it were a rattler about to strike. Charley nodded, and she answered without reading the screen.

"Whose calling?" Her voice was sharp.

"Are you going to let me in?"

"Rebecca! I'm sorry. I thought you were someone else. You're at the front door? And alone?"

"Yes. I got a message about Dave."

Evie pulled the door open. "What kind of a message?"

"Not a good one. That's why I came."

In the kitchen, she handed her phone to Evie, who read the few words, looked at Rebecca and read the message again. "Why would you get this?"

"Maybe because he's been calling me so often." She looked into Evie's eyes, red from crying. "It's true, then?"

Evie nodded. "I gave them the information. They said they'd release him when they found what they were looking for." She glanced at Charley, still on the landline. "She's calling the two police officers in Florida."

CHAPTER NINETEEN

Rebecca hugged Evie close. "I'm so sorry."

"Can you stay, Rebecca?" Charley asked.

"Most of the day."

"I have to go to work, at least for a few hours."

Evie asked, "What did Pellman say?"

"They have a judge's order to open the lockbox. Call me when Rebecca leaves. I'll come home."

Evie started making coffee, her hands shaking so badly that Rebecca took over. "What if they kill him?" Evie asked when she could hold the thought no longer.

"Hey, they didn't kill you. They didn't even hurt you, right? Why would they hurt him now that they've got what they want?"

"I hope you're right, but maybe they didn't kill me because they thought I had the information they wanted."

"Don't think it, Evie. They're safer if they just take the money and run."

"Maybe." Evie sat down.

"I had lunch with Pam last week. She said she misses her conversations with you. Of course, she worries about you."

"It's my fault she moved."

"Well, I wouldn't say it's your fault."

"It's my fault for marrying Ted."

"If you hadn't married Ted, you wouldn't have your kids."

"You're right. I'd have some other kids and none of this would have happened."

Rebecca frowned. "What ifs never got anyone anywhere. Did you tell Angie?"

"God, no. She's busy with her boyfriend. And she would just make everything more difficult."

"Tell me about the island."

Evie smiled. "It was like a piece of paradise…" When she finished, she shrugged. "Until I was kidnapped."

"You might consider seeing a counselor trained to deal with trauma."

"At night, sometimes, I dream bad dreams about being tied up and everybody leaving. Or some guys chasing me. I suppose I'll be dreaming about Dave now. He was tied to a chair when I talked to him. At night he'll be tied to a bed. You can't even scratch an itch. It's maddening. You could go crazy being tied up like that." Evie shook her head and said, "Tell me about John and the kids." She could go crazy thinking about what it must be like for Dave.

"Nothing to tell. They're all fine."

"I wish you could always be here when Charley's gone. Talking helps me forget about Dave. And Georgie isn't much use as protection."

"Well, neither am I. That reminds me. Pam is moving into an apartment and can't find one that allows a dog as big as Max."

"She wants me to take care of Max?"

"Just until she can find a house she can afford. She's been living with her parents. They'll take Max if she can't find anyone else, but they're retired and want to travel."

"What about her girlfriend? Can't she do it?"

"She lives in an apartment too."

"She can rent my house if she wants. Max is a great dog. Could you tell her that for me? I don't know what the condo rules are. Sometimes they only allow cats and small dogs. Tell her I'll call her soon, but don't tell her about Dave."

"Speaking of Charley, you better call her. I have to leave in a few minutes." They stood and hugged for a long time. "I'm so glad you're home, and I'm also worried sick about Dave. But if they turned you loose unharmed, they'll do the same with him. Don't cry, Evie, I shouldn't have brought it up. Now call Charley."

Evie made the call and left a message on Charley's phone.

A few minutes after Rebecca left, the doorbell chimed. Evie ignored it at first, but after it had double-rung three times, she crept through the living room and peeked out the window.

Two police officers were standing on the stoop, their hands on their hips, looking impatient.

Evie unlocked the door and apologized. "I didn't know it was the police."

"We have to go downtown," one officer said.

"Did Jalinsky send you?"

"He's my boss." He met her eyes and looked away.

"I'll call my attorney." She phoned Charley's office, but Charley had left. So, she called her cell and was starting to leave a message when Charley pulled into the driveway.

She walked over to where Evie and the officers stood. "What is it, Officers?"

"Detective Jalinsky wants to see Mrs. Harrington."

"Okay. We'll follow you."

"Wonder what he wants?" Evie said when they were in the car.

"Don't tell him anything. Let me do the talking."

They stopped for a red light. When the light changed and the squad started into the intersection, a dark SUV ran the red light, hit the officers' car, then sped off with a screech of tires.

Charley nearly rear-ended the squad, slamming on the brakes and skidding sideways. After a moment, the officers pursued the SUV.

It all happened so fast that Evie sat stunned, bruised by her seatbelt. "You all right?" Charley asked.

"I think so. Are you?"

"Yeah. But we lost our escort. I guess we proceed on our own."

Jalinsky was waiting, hands on hips, when they got to the police station. He didn't even ask where the officers were. "Sit down, please," he said. "I'll get straight to the point. I hear you have been withholding evidence."

Evie said nothing, although he was looking at her.

Charley said, "I don't think so."

Jalinsky looked angry. "If you know of any evidence regarding Harrington's murder, you need to tell me."

"The only evidence I know of has been reported to the police, just not to anyone in your office."

Jalinsky leaned forward. "What police department? Where?"

Charley told him.

"If you're caught with stolen goods, you will be charged."

"I do know the law."

Jalinsky jerked his office door open and Charley and Evie made their way out of the station through the desks of working policemen and policewomen.

"So, what are you thinking, Evie?" Charley asked.

"Do you think that SUV hit the police car on purpose? And if he did, why? I'm glad we gave Pellman and Babcock the bank and number. I want out of this."

"I'm going to take you home and go to the office. Lock the doors. Maybe Rebecca can come back."

"I forgot to tell you Pam needs a place to keep her dog until she finds an apartment. You remember Max, don't you?"

Charley looked surprised. "The German shepherd? I thought he kept you awake all night, crying for Pam. What about Georgie?"

"Georgie's not afraid of dogs." She remembered the dog crying in the night. "Can you have dogs at the condo?"

"Yes, but there's an extra charge. Maybe a dog is the answer. I worry about you when you're alone."

"I could rent her my house."

"That's an answer," Charley said.

CHAPTER TWENTY

Georgie was patting Evie awake. She pushed him away. She'd slept poorly that night, like every night since Dave was kidnapped. She looked at the clock. Five thirty on the dot. She got up and quietly went down the hall toward the kitchen.

There was something white under Georgie's water bowl. She picked it up while he purred and rubbed against her legs.

It read, MOM, YOU HAVE TO OPEN THE LOCKBOX. DAVE.

She stood, staring at the print, wondering if it was Dave who wrote it. Then she turned to tell Charley and tripped over Georgie. He cried out and she bent to soothe him. "Sorry, sweet boy." She fed him and went back down the hall to the bedroom to wake Charley.

Charley sat up and turned on the light next to the bed. "I'll tell Pellman you have to get into the lockbox. I'll find out if she and Babcock have been there and call you from work."

"All right. I can't function knowing David is tied up somewhere." A bubble of hope blossomed.

When Charley came home, she said the banks were scattered up and down the east coast of Florida, except they weren't all banks. One building had only lockboxes, places to store valuables. A judge had ordered 117 to be opened at the owner's beneficiary's request. Charley had made reservations for her and Evie to fly to Tampa the next day. Evie would need to take one of Ted's death certificates.

"Georgie," Evie said with alarm. "I'll call Rebecca."

Charley said, "I'm calling the locksmith. How are these people getting into the house?"

The locksmith showed up while she was throwing a few clothes in an overnight bag. "I want new locks and deadbolts and an alarm system. All the bells and whistles."

The man, a burly guy, looked her in the eyes. "Break-ins? Did you alert the police?"

She thought of all the break-ins, including the latest when someone left a note. "Somehow, people are getting in when the place is locked up tight. How would that happen?"

"This happens when you're sure everything's locked?"

"Last night someone left a threatening note."

"I'll fix it good."

They went to bed that night with Evie worrying about Dave. Around three, when both were sleeping, the alarm went off.

They jumped out of bed. Charley ran to see who was trying to get in and caught a fleeting sight of a back running away, hair and coat flying. Evie scurried around, arms waving in the air, looking for the code to turn the sound off. Soon there were several half-dressed people at the door along with a police officer.

Charley talked to them, explaining the new system and why she'd had it installed. "We could never stop break-ins before. I saw someone running away when I got to the door." The sound was mercifully stilled.

After a few questions and a lot of talk among them, they all left, including the officer.

Evie was listening nearby.

When they both went back to bed, there was no sleeping at first. Evie was rigid, waiting for the alarm to go off. They did succumb because they both startled awake when the radio came on.

They drove to the airport in the Jeep. Charley kept looking at her mirrors. Finally, Evie said, "Don't tell me we're being followed."

"Yep. No point in trying to lose him now." She handed the garage door opener to Evie. "We can't leave it in here. Put it in your bag, will you?"

"Did you take the other one that was in the Subaru?"

"I did. It occurred to me that's how they were getting in."

"But wouldn't we hear the garage door opening and closing?"

"Maybe it wasn't opened all the way, just enough to get in."

Evie looked in her sideview mirror and took note of the vehicle behind her. "The one right behind us?"

"Think so."

"Let's park and see if it passes."

The car was an older Ford. A policeman waved as he passed and then parked, waiting for them to go on. They did and he continued to follow.

"Is he on our side, or theirs?" Evie asked.

"I think we have to trust that he's on ours."

CHAPTER TWENTY-ONE

As soon as they were in the air, Evie fell asleep. She awakened with a jolt when they landed in Milwaukee. They had to change to a larger plane and had less than an hour to get to the gate.

When they landed in Tampa, they headed to the car rentals. A line had already formed at Alamo where they had reserved a car. A half hour later they were on their way to Englewood where they met Officers Pellman and Babcock in the parking lot of a Walmart. They followed the officers to a one-story brick building with no discernable windows. It looked nothing like a bank. A thin man with wavy brown hair and a nice suit opened the door, examined the judge's order carried by the officers and the death certificate, marriage license and driver's license that Evie had brought.

The man grunted and waved everyone but Evie and Pellman to chairs in the hallway. The two women followed him down a long hall that ended at a door. Evie assumed the back door led to a parking lot. Before they got that far, they stopped at a room with large lockboxes. He unlocked 117 with one key and then drilled into the other lock, pulling it out on the end of the drill bit. He put the closed box he'd pulled on a shelf in a small room and shut Evie in with it.

She thought Pellman was supposed to be with her. She opened the door but saw no one, so she shut it. Perhaps Pellman had gone back for something. She opened the lid and slowly began removing its contents. Her heart pounded erratically. She was so nervous she could barely concentrate. Where had Ted gotten all this money? Stacks of clean, crisp bills. Surely, the numbers were recorded somewhere. How was he ever going to be able to use it?

She began packing a zippered bag with clean one-thousand-dollar bills, keeping tabs as she went on a notepad. At the bottom of the box, she uncovered clear bags of white powdery stuff. Heroin probably. Oh, Ted, she thought. How had he managed to squirrel away over two million dollars in cash and who knew how much in drugs? No wonder guys were breaking into the house and condo and following her everywhere.

She opened the door of the little room, thinking about the next step. She had been told to leave the bag at a storage place called Bounce and ask them to hold the bag for Jack Kendall, who would pick it up. David was to be released in Lettuce Lake Park off I-75. She stopped dead, slow to switch gears, eyeing the hand holding a gun for a moment before raising her gaze to the face of the man with the wavy hair.

He reached for the bag and for one stupid moment she tried to hang on. David, she thought, as the man jerked it away from her and backed out the door. She heard the key turn in the lock.

She should have known it wouldn't be easy. She fought off tears, hoping that the wavy-haired man had David and intended to release him. She pounded on the door and shouted for what seemed at least an hour. She was going hoarse when the door opened, and she nearly fell into a strange man's arms.

"Who are you?" And then she saw the others behind him. "What?"

"This is Bob Bitterman," Pellman said. "He's the caretaker here. The other guy hit him on the head, tied him up and locked him up in another room. He did the same to me. The others heard him yelling and set him loose. We didn't hear you till they found me."

Bitterman opened the end door. Only one car was in the parking lot. "We hired this guy to work nights. He gave his name as Jack Kendall."

"That's who was supposed to pick up the bag from Bounce," Evie said.

"Yeah. Well, you can bet that Jack Kendall isn't his name," Bitterman said, "even though his credentials checked out. I wonder if there is a Jack Kendall."

"Let's go to Lettuce Lake. Maybe Dave will be there," Evie croaked. He had to be. She wouldn't be able to endure it if he wasn't.

Pellman called the local police, gave them her ID, and asked them to send a couple of officers and an ambulance to the Ballmount address. Babcock left with Charley and Evie. Lettuce Lake was not far away. They parked in the lot and walked toward the park building. Through the open doors on the rear porch, Evie saw a slender man leaning on the railing. His brown hair trailed down to his T-shirt where it ended in a little flip. His back muscles bulged.

With a small cry, Evie ran toward him. She touched his back. He turned and embraced her. "Mom, what happened? Are you all right?"

She was sobbing, her nose running. She found a tissue in her capri pocket and blew her nose. She patted him, checking to make sure he was all right. "They didn't hurt you?"

He took her hands in his. Burns encircled his wrists. "What was this all about? I was just walking to Dad's car when someone grabbed me."

She never should have let him use that car. "I'll tell you later. There is a police officer who wants to talk to you."

Charley and Babcock approached them.

"We need to go to the police station," Babcock said.

Dave looked confused and then smiled—eyes bright, teeth white, one arm around his mother. "Guess so. Can't wait to find out what's going on."

At the police station, Babcock and another officer questioned Dave. He later told his mother and Charley what they asked him and the answers he gave.

How was he kidnapped? He was shoved into a car outside his apartment. Where was he taken? He didn't know. How did he get to Florida? By car. Was he hurt? He held out his wrists. Could he describe his kidnappers? He shook his head. "They covered my eyes or wore masks."

"Someone took you to Lettuce Lake."

"Yeah. I never saw him. He untied me and pushed me out of the car and drove off. By the time I pulled off the blindfold, he was gone."

"All right. You can go. We'll call if we need anything else."

Dave walked out into the sunshine where Evie and Charley were waiting. Evie and David climbed in the back seat of the rental car. Charley drove toward the airport.

"I thought I was going to die, and then I thought Mom was dead. That was the worst." Dave looked at his mother, and she reached for his hand. "It's all been so confusing. What aren't you telling me?"

So, his mother told him.

His jaw dropped, literally. "Dad hid millions of dollars? Where did he get that kind of money?"

"We followed the money to get you released."

"You knew about the money?"

"No. All we had was the name of a bank and lockbox number."

Dave stared at her, his light brown eyes turning dark. "Why didn't I know?"

"And what would you have done? I didn't want to put you or Angie in danger." She remembered those long days tied to a chair. Dave kept Evie busy answering his questions. He seemed astonished by what she had to say, almost speechless.

Finally, he said, "I never figured Dad for a crook. I mean, he was a lot of things, but a criminal? Were you surprised, Mom?"

"Yes. But when guys kept breaking into the house in the middle of the night, looking for something, I figured that he'd hidden something valuable. Or at least he knew where it was. And then I found the note with the bank and lockbox number. You were kidnapped. I gave the information to one of them who called, thinking they'd let you go. But they wanted me to get the stuff out of the lockbox. And now they have the money and dope and I have you. The cops will have to find them. I hope I never have to worry about someone breaking in again."

"But some of that money belongs to you, Mom. Don't you want it?"

"I want to be left alone."

Charley drove into the car rental return and parked. After unloading their overnight bags, they headed for the Alamo rental to turn in their paperwork. By the time they'd gone through security and were at the United gate, the plane was in the process of boarding.

On the drive to Charley's condo from Outagamie International, Evie began to explain why they were not going to her and Dave's home. "It wasn't safe at our place, so Georgie and I moved in with Charley."

"What about Rebecca?" he asked.

Evie hadn't the slightest idea how to tell him about Charley and her. "Charley doesn't have a dog. But the break-ins continued. So, we went to an island off Florida where Charley's family has a vacation home. That's where we met the two officers we just talked to. That's where I was kidnapped too."

Dave looked lost. "Let's go back to why you left our home."

"Because it wasn't safe. I was always getting knocked over the head or tied up."

"Where were the cops?"

"Out front."

They were pulling into Charley's garage.

"Whoa," he said. "I think I should stay at home."

"Why don't you stay tonight, Dave. Then if you want to go home tomorrow…" Charley shrugged.

Dave walked around inside, hands on his hips. "Nice place."

"I'll show you to your room," Evie said.

He whistled in appreciation when he saw the huge bed, private bath, the TV, the radio and the bookcase full of books. "Living in luxury, Mom. Where are you sleeping?"

She felt her face getting hot under his gaze.

The corner of his mouth twitched. "You too, Mom?"

"Yes," she said, frozen in place. She'd have to be honest sometime. Might as well be now. "Me too. Never would have guessed it."

He sat down on the bed and stared at her. "What am I going to tell Angie?"

"Nothing about that."

"Then you'll have to." He barked a laugh and then began to whoop. When he could talk again, he said, "My own mother."

"What's for supper?" he asked.

"I'll take your order. We're getting takeout."

"He guessed?" Charley whispered in bed that night.

"He's gay, you know," Evie whispered back.

"No, I didn't know."

"Ted made it tough for him. He was only fourteen when Ted figured it out. Ted called him a sissy, although he's not a sissy. He loves wildlife and the environment. He's helped tag eagles and bears. Ted always favored Angie. She was his girl. But Dave and Angie are close despite everything."

"So, who's going to tell Angie?"

"Maybe Rebecca."

"Coward," Charley teased.

"You bet."

Evie had sent Rebecca an email on the way home the day before. She threw her arms around Evie when she let her in the next morning, after setting down Georgie's kennel.

"Where is the golden boy?" she asked, going off to embrace Dave.

"They let me go, after Mom found the money."

Evie put a cup of coffee in front of Rebecca as she said, "Ah. That's what was hidden."

"Millions," Dave said. "I wonder if Dad ever thought about what might happen to Mom and to me?"

Everyone was quiet for a few moments, until Evie said, "Hey, this is a celebration of sorts."

Charley was standing, drinking coffee. She was dressed in the suit she'd had on when Evie first went into her office. The blouse matched her eyes. She wore low heels. "I wish I could stay, but I have to go to work. Thanks for taking care of Georgie, Rebecca. Dave, I hope you're still here when I get home."

"Hey, thanks for letting me stay."

"Any time," Rebecca said.

Evie followed her to the door, stood on her toes and gave Charley a kiss. Even so, Charley had to bend over. The others clapped.

"You want to tell me what happened, Dave," Rebecca asked.

He did and she said, "It must have been pretty scary."

"Yeah. No scarier than it was for Mom, I expect." Dave looked at Evie. 'I don't like to think about how scared you must have been, Mom."

"I was terrified at first, but then they didn't do anything to me except tie me up. So, then I was bored, but there was always an edge of fear that one of them might get too impatient because I couldn't tell them anything. Did I tell you how I was rescued?"

So, there was that to talk about.

"Thank God!" Rebecca said and sat down at the table "I hope things settle down now. I can't take much more of this." She pulled a bottle of champagne out of her shoulder bag. "This is too monumental for coffee." She pulled the cork out with a satisfying pop and hiss and poured champagne into the glasses Evie put on the table.

Evie rested a hand on her shoulder as she sipped from the still bubbling drink. "Nor can I."

CHAPTER TWENTY-TWO

Someone knocked on the door. "Who could that be?" Evie asked, annoyed. She opened it to see Detective Jalinsky and one of the police officers on the doorstep.

"What do you want now?

"Evelyn Harrington, you're under arrest for the murder of Theodore Harrington," Jalinsky said and read her Miranda Rights. "Put the handcuffs on," he said to the officer.

She stared at him, uncomprehending.

"Wait a minute," Rebecca said. "As you know, she has an attorney, who is on her way. "I suggest you wait."

"And who are you?" Jalinsky's mouth curled.

"A friend who knows she didn't kill her husband."

Dave had also jumped to his feet. "Yeah. She didn't do anything. She's a victim."

"I think you're both drunk. Handcuff her."

The officer fumbled with the handcuffs. "Maybe we should wait for her attorney. She might turn herself in."

Jalinsky turned on the officer. "Who do you think you are?" he shouted.

They were attracting a few people, who moved in closer.

Charley's tires screamed as she pulled into the driveway. She ran to the front door, which was open. "Thanks for the heads up, Rebecca." She turned to Jalinsky. "What's going on, Detective?"

"This woman is under arrest for murder. We're taking her in for questioning."

"Whose murder?" Charley looked as disbelieving as she sounded.

"Theodore Harrington."

"Don't say a word, unless I tell you it's okay," Charley said on the way over to the station.

The mellow of the champagne had worn off. Evie didn't want to spend the night in jail. What if the women in the cell ganged up on her? She wasn't sure she could stand up to even one woman.

"Don't worry, Evie. We'll make bail and you'll be out of there just like that."

After she surrendered everything except her clothes and had been frisked, Jalinsky steered the two women into a room equipped with a table and chairs and a recording system.

Charley said, "What's going on, Detective? You know that Evie was working the day her husband was killed. You know her house was broken into numerous times, that she was even attacked and ended up in the hospital. She was also kidnapped."

Jalinsky ignored Charley and asked Evie if she had some of the loot from the lockbox.

Evie had stuffed that first thousand into her pocket before the wavy-haired guy had made off with the rest. She looked at Charley.

Charley slapped paper-taped money on the table. "She put this stack of ten one-hundred-dollar bills into her pocket before the man pretending to work there took the rest."

"Why did you do that? Why did you take the evidence, Mrs. Harrington?"

"There was over two million in the box. She couldn't believe it was real."

Evie nodded. "I was going to give it to Pellman. She's a policewoman. But the man took the bag and locked me in the room. I didn't care if he made off with it. I thought maybe the guys who were looking for the money would finally leave me alone. Guess I was wrong." She glared at Jalinsky.

"You killed your husband for that money, didn't you?" Jalinsky said.

It felt like a slap. "Charley told you I was working when he was killed."

"The imperfect alibi. You could always pay someone to kill him."

Evie looked at him with contempt. "I don't have to talk to you." She stood. "You're a fool."

"Take her to a cell."

Charley was protesting there wasn't enough evidence to charge her with anything. Her voice faded as the officer led Evie away.

"I don't believe you killed anyone," the officer whispered.

"Tell him that," Evie snapped.

"It's only for one night. Tomorrow you can post bail."

Evie looked at the gray walls. "You should paint these a brighter color."

They turned a corner and he opened a barred door and led her inside. She looked around wildly at the four bunks, the toilet in a corner, the sink next to it, the bars facing the hall.

The officer locked the door and said to the guard, "Take good care of this lady."

A few minutes later, a very upset Charley stood outside the cell. "Are you all right?"

"No, I'm not all right. I didn't do anything. Why am I locked up? Why not the guys who broke into the house? Why not the ones who kidnapped me?" She was beside herself with anger, stomping around the cell.

"Jalinsky has to blame someone." Charley reached through the bars and the guard stopped her. "I'll call Pellman and Babcock and find out if the kidnappers have been charged."

"I don't even have a book to read. What do people do in here?"

"I can't stay, Evie. I'll be back in the morning."

Evie lay on one of the beds but jumped up again after a few minutes. She marched around the cell, counting her steps. They had taken her watch, so she had no idea of time. Eventually, dinner came. She took one look at the tray with its soupy-looking meat, lumpy mashed potatoes, a pile of peas and a piece of white bread and set it on the lower bed across the cell.

She heard a commotion down the hall. A woman screamed, "I didn't do nothing! Let me go!"

The guard opened Evie's cell door, unlocked the handcuffs and released the woman. She had bleach-blond crimped hair, huge blue eyes encircled with black eyelashes that were so long they couldn't be her own. Her breasts were bursting out of her low-cut pullover and her skirt barely covered her crotch. She wore lacy stockings and incredibly high heels.

"Why are you staring at me?" she yelled at Evie.

"I'm not," Evie protested, although she had been.

"Mine is the oldest profession in the world. Do you know what that is?" She was in Evie's face.

Evie backed away. "Yes."

"Of course, you probably only have sex on your back with your husband."

"My husband was murdered," Evie said.

"Did you kill him? He probably deserved it."

Evie shook her curls. "No. I found him, though." She sat down on the bed.

"Yeah? Did someone shoot him? Or stab him?"

"Someone hit him over the head and slit his throat. I didn't even notice he was dead at first."

She sat down next to Evie. "Tell me about it."

Close up, the makeup didn't hide the wrinkles. "You don't want to hear the whole story. It's long."

"I do. I do want to hear. We got all night. My name is Sunshine because of my blond hair. What's yours?"

"Evie." Sunshine's perfume was so strong that it made Evie's eyes water.

"We got all night. I'll just sit here and listen."

"Why don't you lie up there. Then we can both lie down."

"Nighttime is my working time. But okay. I have this night off." She clambered up to the top bunk. "You can start now."

"Well, I called 911 and Detective Jalinsky showed up. Do you know him? He's the one who thinks I killed Ted."

"Ain't never heard of him."

She was partway through her tale when the guard opened the door and another woman, dressed somewhat like Sunshine, joined them.

"This is Lilac, Evie. She's a friend of mine. You should hear this story, Lilac. They're framing Evie for the murder of her husband. Start over, Evie. Take the weight off your feet and listen, Lilac."

Lilac was tall with dark hair. Her eyes were lined with black, which stood out on her pale face.

It seemed to Evie that she talked all night. Every once in a while one of the women would ask a question.

"Why you travelin' with your lawyer?" Lilac asked.

"She was trying to protect me."

"Never heard of that before."

"Shhh," Sunshine said.

And Evie continued. They were now on the island in Florida.

"Your lawyer is rich," Lilac commented.

When Evie talked about the kidnapping, Lilac got up on an elbow and Sunshine leaned over the side of the bunk.

"Did they rape you?" Sunshine asked.

"No. They only wanted what was in the lockbox, but I'd just discovered the note with the bank and lockbox number. I couldn't remember what it said."

"Would you've told them?" Lilac asked.

"I don't know."

When she told how Charley and her mother rescued her, they beat their hands on the sides of their beds. "Ain't that amazing!" Sunshine said.

"Amazing, yeah!" Lilac chimed in.

"Your lawyer and her mother did that?" Sunshine exclaimed.

"They use rubber bullets. Those kidnappers crawled back to the cottage." Evie laughed. "The cops arrested them."

"They didn't hurt them really bad?" Lilac asked.

"Nah. They spit the dirt in front of them. Charley's mom doesn't want to injure anyone."

"They sound like a couple of dykes. Tough," Lilac said.

She pondered that before agreeing. "You don't have to be a dyke to be tough." As she continued, she noticed the guard was leaning against the bars, listening.

Before morning there were three more women in the cell, all garbed in extra-short skirts and revealing tops. All with lots of makeup and long dyed hair. Sunshine and Lilac were telling them Evie's story.

Evie heard their voices as she continued to drift off to sleep.

"Wake up, honey. Time to see the judge. Your lawyer lady is here."

Evie opened her eyes to see Sunshine leaning over her. She had to urinate. She went to the corner and the women turned their backs in front of her to shield her from curious eyes. "Hey, thanks," she said and washed her hands before running her fingers through her curls.

Sunshine said, "Thank you for getting us through the night." She hugged Evie and Evie hugged her back.

Lilac embraced her next. "Get your ass out of here."

"Good luck," Evie said, "to all of you."

Charley raised an eyebrow, and Lilac asked, "You one of them so good with a gun?"

Charley's mouth twisted into a smile. "My mother's better."

A thin cheer followed Evie out the barred door. She waved and blew a kiss.

"Don't let them numbskulls frame you!" Lilac yelled.

"Yeah, you didn't do nothing wrong," Sunshine hollered.

"What the hell?" Charley asked, as they walked away.

Evie smiled. "I told my story."

"Next they'll be coming over for coffee."

"Hey, I could meet Sunshine and Lilac for coffee." She started to turn around.

Charley grabbed her arm and turned her back. "Right now, we're getting you out of here."

The judge looked over her glasses at Ned Brown, the prosecutor. "On what grounds do you want to refuse bail?"

"The suspect fled to Florida after the murder."

Anxiety made it impossible for Evie to sit still. She was trying very hard to put her trust in Charley and keep her own mouth shut.

The judge turned to Charley, who said, "The suspect was away when her husband was killed. Her house was broken into numerous times. She was knocked out and tied up by men looking for money her husband hid. She went to Florida to be safe, but in Florida she was kidnapped, also by men looking for the money the suspect's husband hid. She had no idea where that money was."

The prosecutor and Charley verbally sparred while Evie squirmed. If she had to go back to that cell, she hoped Sunshine and Lilac would be there. What she desperately wanted was a shower.

Finally, the judge raised her hands. "Enough. I don't understand why you want to deny bail to this person, Ned. I am going to release her on her own recognizance. Next case."

Jalinsky, who had been sitting in the first row, looked stunned. He got up, turned on his heel and left the room.

Still shaky, Evie walked out of the courthouse with Charley. After picking up Evie's belongings and heading toward the parking ramp where Charley's car was parked, Evie heard her name called. She turned and saw Sunshine and Lilac running toward her. "Wait, Charley," she said.

"Hey, you want a ride home?" Evie asked.

"Nah. Just want to know what the judge said." The women looked older in the sunlight.

Evie told her. "What about you two?"

Lilac said, "John took care of our bail." She jerked a thumb at a guy at the end of the block.

They waved goodbye and Evie and Charley entered the ramp and drove home. "Was it horrible for you?"

"Until Sunshine got there. I suppose that guy who got them out is their pimp?"

"I expect so." Charley braked before turning onto the street. "My mother can hardly contain her anger at Jalinsky."

"Do you think he really believes I killed Ted?"

"I think he's angry because you cut him out of the money."

"By not telling him the bank and lockbox number?"

"Yep."

"Should I have told him?"

"Maybe, to be safe."

"But you didn't suggest that."

"You didn't ask me."

Evie sank back in the seat. "I just wanted to be left alone."

"I know." Charley reached for her hand and squeezed it. "You're not going to jail, honey."

But she now knew that Charley might not be able to keep that promise.

CHAPTER TWENTY-THREE

In bed, Charley took Evie's book away from her. "I feel badly about your spending the night in jail. I felt so helpless."

"I don't think it was your fault, if that makes you feel better. I'm trying to think of it as a learning experience."

"I was awake all night, worrying about you." Charley's mouth, always so soft and pliant, shot desire through Evie. She rolled on top of her and kissed her lips, her neck, her breasts, her belly, and the inside of her thighs in a burst of sexual energy.

Charley laughed and pulled her back up, face-to-face, then tugged lightly on Evie's nightshirt. "Take it off."

For a few moments, they lay pressed together, Charley breathing into Evie's ear while Evie breathed into her neck. Then Charley flipped Evie onto her back, covered her with kisses before straddling her and gently spreading her legs.

When Evie felt the soft caress of tongue, she gasped and pulled Charley's hips down.

Afterward, as they lay side by side, catching their collective breath, Evie said, "Well, that was worth going to jail for."

Charley looked at her. "You don't have to go to jail. You just have to tell me you want it."

Angie called the Friday of the Fourth of July weekend. "Hey, Mom, I'm coming home."

Dave had already informed Evie of this. He had returned to Milwaukee and his apartment. He was picking Angie up and taking her to Charley's condo, although no one had told her that her mother was living there. Evie had suggested Dave bring her up-to-date, so it wouldn't come as a shock when they arrived.

They showed up at six. Charley was still at work, trying to catch up on time lost. They came through the garage door, arguing loudly. Charley had given Dave the code, so that he could go in and out when he was staying with them.

Evie cringed, listening to their voices. She took a deep breath and faced her children as they entered the kitchen. "Hey, honey, you're looking good." She was always surprised at how fresh and pretty her daughter was. She held out her arms. Angie hesitated before moving into them for a short hug.

Dave embraced his mother and whispered in her ear, "Hang in there. She'll come around."

"What are you whispering, Dave?" Angie asked. She set her weekend bag down and jammed her hands onto her hips.

Dave smiled at his sister. "I just told Mom you'd come around."

"To her living in someone else's house, instead of ours? No, I won't."

Evie's gaze shifted from one to the other. She cleared her throat. "Why don't I show you to your room, Angie."

Angie huffed but followed her mother down the hall to the room across from Charley's. It was an appealing room with a small bathroom attached. The windows looked out at a green space between condos. Angie put her bag on the floor and looked around.

"Do you like it?" Evie asked.

"I like my own bedroom better. What are you doing here, Mom? Who owns this place?"

"Charley Webster. You met her once at the offices of Farley and Webster. She's my attorney." Evie studied her daughter.

"But why do you live here?"

"It wasn't safe to live at home. Get settled and come to the kitchen. We'll talk."

Angie dropped her bag and followed her mother. "Why wasn't it safe?"

"Sit down, honey. Do you want a cup of coffee?"

"I want a beer."

"We don't have any beer. We have wine and vodka and gin." Evie studied her daughter. She remembered her stumbling drunk, sometimes combative, other times silly or quiet. "Let's wait for Charley to have drinks."

"Tell me why it isn't safe to live at home?" Angie persisted.

It probably was safe now. "People kept breaking in during the night after your dad died."

Angie's smooth brow furrowed. "What?"

"They were looking for information leading to a lot of money. Now they have the money, but I still don't feel safe there. Besides, I'm thinking of renting it to a friend."

"Who?" Dave asked.

"Our former neighbor, Pam. She hasn't found an apartment that allows large dogs. She has a lovely German shepherd." She may as well include the renting with the rest of the story.

"Mom's out of jail on bond," Dave said.

Angie sucked in air. "How do you know that and I don't?"

"You've been busy with your boyfriend and work. When was the last time you were home?"

Angie jerked as if she'd been slapped.

Evie shot Dave a look that said *shut up*. "Hon, it's such a long story. I didn't want to send it in an email." She was tired of explaining everything.

"But why were you in jail?"

"I'm accused of killing your dad," she said.

"That's crazy," Angie said. "How did that happen?" She looked from Dave to her mother.

"Not sure." And she wasn't.

"Well, I think Detective Jalinsky was pissed about losing the money and drugs and blamed it on your mother." Charley stood in the doorway, her briefcase in one hand, her blond hair falling out of its French twist. "Hello, Angie. Nice to see you again."

Angie stood up, her body rigid with fury. "My mom's not a dyke."

Charley looked over the young woman's head at Evie and raised her eyebrows, as if to say *Where did this come from?*

Appalled, Evie asked, "Angie, how could you?"

"No, it's okay, but tell me what you have against lesbians?" Charley asked.

"Would you want your mother to be a lesbian?"

"Well, I wouldn't want her to leave my dad, but other than that, I wouldn't care. If you saw my mom in action, you'd think she was a lesbian. Right, Evie?"

"She and Charley rescued me after I'd been kidnapped."

Angie spun around. "Kidnapped! Why didn't I know, Dave?"

Dave had been standing very still, trying to stay out of the way of his sister's anger. He said, "Because I didn't know, but they rescued me when I was kidnapped."

"Your mother rescued you, Dave, when she told the bad guys the name of the bank and lockbox," Charley said.

He smiled at his mom. "You gave up all that money because of me?"

"And drugs," Evie said. "I didn't actually give any of it up because it wasn't mine, as you know, Dave."

"I'm going to change my clothes and then have a drink. Anyone want to join me?" Charley asked.

"I do," Angie and Dave said in unison.

"You're not twenty-one yet, Dave."

"Oh, come on, Mom. I'll be twenty-one in less than two months."

Charley padded in on bare feet, dressed in old jeans and a T-shirt. Evie handed her a gin and tonic and sat down with a glass of pinot noir. Dave had brought beer in a cooler and he and Angie each held one.

When the doorbell rang, Dave jumped to his feet. 'Who's that?"

"I don't know," Charley said. "Why don't you go see?"

Evie tensed, afraid it was Jalinsky coming to take her back to jail, but when she heard Rebecca talking to Dave, she hurried to greet her but then stopped to listen.

"Angie's here and she's being bitchy about Mom being a lesbian."

"Is your mom a lesbian?"

"Am I gay?"

Rebecca laughed.

"You know, if she was going to be a lesbian, I wanted you to be her partner."

"Well, I suppose you mean that as a compliment, Dave, but I think Charley is perfect for her."

They had stopped and dropped their voices. Dave said, "She is, but you've always been like a second mother."

"Aww. That's sweet. I've always felt that way too. You're all grown up now. You need a boyfriend."

"I've got one. I'm going to bring him home next time."

"Let me know when because I want to meet him."

When she stepped out of the den's doorway, Rebecca said. "You're a snoop." She put an arm around Evie.

They had to separate to get through the kitchen door. Angie ran to Rebecca and gave her a big hug. "I hoped I'd see you."

Evie looked on with envy, wondering if her daughter would ever be so glad to see her. She caught Charley eyeing her from the table.

Charley raised her drink. "Rebecca, what do you imbibe?"

"A glass of wine would be nice," she said, nodding at Evie's pinot noir.

When they were all sitting down, Angie asked Rebecca, "Did you know Mom and Dave were kidnapped and Mom was in jail?"

"Terrible, isn't it? I wanted to ask your mom what being in jail was like."

"It was grim until I met Sunshine and Lilac. I met Sunshine first and she cheered me up."

"What were they in for?" Angie asked.

Charley said, "Hookers. They're hookers."

"Were the johns in jail or the men who paid to have sex with them?" Angie asked angrily. When everyone looked surprised, she said, "Well, it's just not fair. Women always get the short end of the stick."

Charley cleared her throat, Evie looked proud, and Rebecca said, "That's very true, Angie."

"Hey, sis. There's something to fight for: Women's Rights."

"Yeah. You're lucky to be a guy," Angie said.

"Don't bite me. I agree with you."

"We all do," Charley said.

"Your daughter is a women's libber," Charley whispered in bed that night.

"I'm not surprised. She never tolerated any guy who didn't treat her equally. It doesn't make any sense, her attitude toward lesbians."

"That's because you're her mother. She probably has lesbian friends."

"She does. One of her roommates. Maybe she's afraid someone is going to think she's gay. People can be touchy about that."

"Nah," Charley said, kissing her. "I was touchy in high school and college. Women athletes. Lots of people think we're dykes."

"Well, you were."

"I know, but I was young and wanted to be like the other kids. I was ashamed of being gay."

"I never even knew I was gay," Evie said.

But in retrospect, she realized she'd been in love with Rebecca.

CHAPTER TWENTY-FOUR

The phone rang as Charley was making coffee. She grabbed the receiver. Everyone else was sleeping. Who the hell would call at six a.m.?

"Hi, it's Pellman. I just realized what time it is where you are. I'm so sorry, but I've got good news."

"Hi. This is Charley. You didn't wake me up. I'm getting ready for work. Evie's asleep. How are you, anyway?"

"Good. Really good. We caught the person who stole the lockbox money and he's talking."

"That's great news. Let me get Evie on the other line. She'll want to hear this. Hang on." She hurried down the hall, picked up the bedroom phone and shook Evie gently by the shoulder. "Pellman is on the phone." She handed Evie the receiver and put the kitchen phone to her ear. "I just woke her up so she might be a little fuzzy."

"Pellman, what's going on?" Evie sounded very wide awake.

"We caught the guy who took the lockbox contents. And he talked. So far, we've picked up four guys and there are more, including three from your town. One is a police detective. He was arrested, but he's out on bail."

"Am I dreaming this?" Evie asked.

"Is the detective's name Jason Jalinsky?" Charley asked.

"Do you know him?"

"Oh, yes, we know him," Charley said.

"Jalinsky arrested me last week. Accused me of murdering my husband, the one who hid all that money and drugs."

Charley heard the sharp intake of breath. "You're kidding. Maybe he killed your husband."

"It's possible."

Charley said, "We suspected Jalinsky was somehow involved because he was just too interested in the case. He had to have other cases. We caught one guy who broke in the house, and the first one here was Jalinsky with no back-up. He dragged the man off before he had a chance to say much of anything."

"How did you catch the man who took the bag with all the money and drugs?" Evie asked.

"After the theft was publicized, someone in an apartment building found the empty bag in one of those big trash bins outside the building while looking for something his wife threw out. Nick Scarbody lived in that apartment building. He has a record. It was in our jurisdiction, so we took him in for questioning and he talked."

"Why did he talk?" Evie asked.

"He had a lot of unexplained money in his apartment. He'll get off a little easier because he turned the others in. Got to go now. I wanted you two to know in case Jalinsky or Boyd Whipley or Gordon Skinadore show up. One of them may have killed Evie's husband."

Evie followed Charley into the kitchen and finished making the coffee. "If Jalinsky comes over, do I let him in?"

"No. I think I'll stay home till the detective is picked up for questioning. It's the weekend anyway."

"How will we know?" Evie asked.

"I'll find out."

A sleepy-looking Dave showed up, poured a cup of coffee and plunked down at the table. "Ang is taking a shower."

The doorbell rang. Charley met Evie's eyes and shook her head.

"I'll get it," David said and started to get up.

Evie put her hand on his shoulder. "No, son." At his puzzled look, she said, "Whoever it is can call us. We're not opening the door until we know who is on the other side."

The ringing turned into pounding about the time Angie showed up and poured a cup of coffee. "Why aren't you answering the door?"

"We don't know who it is," her mother said.

"Well, there's one way to find out." When she put her cup on the table next to Dave, he took her hand and pulled her down. "What did you do that for?"

"Don't get all huffy. Mom and Charley don't want to answer the door."

They heard glass breaking and Charley ran to the bedroom and came out with her handgun.

"Go to one of your rooms," Evie said, grabbing the phone and dialing 911, but Angie and Dave sat as if frozen.

"Well, hello, Evie. Put that phone back on the hook right now." When she slowly complied, he asked, "Why aren't you answering the door? You can send me a bill for the window glass. Are these charming young people your children?"

Charley stood in the doorway and raised the gun, pointing it at Jalinsky. "Put the gun down, Jalinsky."

Jalinsky fired his gun and Charley did the same. The sound reverberated around the room, making Evie and Angie jump. His bullet hit her in the thigh, and hers struck him in the shoulder. He dropped his gun. But he was firing real bullets. She did not drop hers, but she momentarily lost her focus. Blood spurted out of the wound.

Jalinsky bent to pick up his weapon as Dave dove for it. The detective knocked him out with the butt of the revolver. Then he shot Charley in the arm as she aimed again, and she fell, splattering blood.

Evie, who had been momentarily stunned, ran toward Jalinsky.

Angie screamed. "No, Mom. He'll kill you."

Her daughter's scream apparently brought her to her senses, and she stopped and backed away.

"Go get that toy gun away from your friend."

Charley lifted the weapon and aimed. Her gaze was wavering as she pulled the trigger. She heard Jalinsky shout, and she jerked as a bullet grazed her neck.

"Charley," Evie said.

"That son of a bitch," Charley murmured. "Too bad you can't shoot."

"Charley, just lie still. You'll bleed to death otherwise," Evie said, taking the gun and throwing it under the table. She looked at Jalinsky. "If she dies, you'll be in for murder. You need to let me help her."

He said to Angie, "Kick that gun my way, girl."

Angie kicked it as far from him as she could. It skidded to the other side of the fridge. "You'll just have to get it yourself."

He walked over and was picking the gun up when Dave jumped him from behind. Jalinsky grunted and took a few running steps but then he hit the wall. He turned and aimed the gun at Dave, his arm shaking.

The bullet hit a glancing blow in Dave's side. "Don't make me kill you, kid."

Dave threw up on Jalinsky's feet and fell.

Evie screamed. "You killed him. You murdered my son, you fucking bastard."

"I didn't kill him. I nearly missed him, because of that friend of yours. Go fix her up. Stop the bleeding."

Evie checked on Dave, who said his head hurt. She saw no blood and went to Charley, who was drifting in and out of consciousness. "I have to get some towels and gauze. Lots of it."

"Go get whatever you need. Don't forget your kids are in here with me."

She came out of the bathroom with all the gauze she could find and an armful of towels. Carefully, she rolled Charley over.

"Where? Tell me where?" she asked when she met Charley's eyes.

Charley pointed at her thigh. "Stop that," she whispered, and Evie wrapped four rolls of gauze above the wound and tied it. She put some on the wound, but it immediately bled through. "There." Charley pointed at her arm, and Evie wrapped it above and on the wound. She put gauze on Charley's neck.

She started mopping up the blood with the towels. "Let me know if they're too tight."

"Leave the bitch there," Jalinsky said.

"I can't tell if the bleeding has stopped if I don't clean the floor," Evie said.

Charley was shaking with cold. "Blanket," she said.

"I have to get her a blanket. She could die of shock." Evie stood stubbornly over Charley.

"Get one then." Jalinsky was shaking too.

Evie put the blanket from their bed over Charley, who winced. "I paid five hundred for that," she whispered.

"You're worth it." Evie could no longer swallow the tears.

"Come over and sit at the table," Jalinsky said. His voice was fading.

Evie sat next to Angie, angry tears dribbling down her face, meeting the snot from her nose. Angie's hand crept over hers. Evie grabbed a napkin and stopped the snot. "If anybody dies, you could spend your life in prison."

"I'm a cop. Cops don't spend their lives in prison." With his gun trained on them, he poured himself a cup of coffee. "How about two pieces of toast? I haven't eaten today."

"I'll do it, Mom," Evie's daughter said. The bread and butter were already on the table. The toaster was on the other side of the fridge. She walked past her brother, laid out on the floor, his face the color of dough, his side blood-stained. She put the bread in the toaster and pushed it down. Jalinsky's gun moved back and forth between her and her mother.

It was then they heard sirens, shrill shrieks rising and falling, invading the quiet morning.

Jalinsky downed the coffee in two gulps and stuffed the toast into his mouth. He looked at Evie. "Write this down."

She grabbed a pencil and a paper napkin. Jalinsky gave her a familiar number. "Call my wife. Tell her I love her and will be in touch."

"Why should I do that?"

He was on his way down the hall. "Because you're a woman. Do it for her." He tossed Charley's gun and jumped out the window in Dave's room.

Evie ran to Charley, whose eyes were closed. "Try to get the blood off the floor," she murmured. "Fix the window. Okay? How is everyone?"

"Dave has a concussion. Jalinsky hit him over the head when he dove for his gun. A bullet also grazed his side. You're the one who's really hurt. Where is your insurance card?"

"In my wallet in my briefcase," she murmured. "Why do you sound so angry?"

"Why do you always have to play rescuer?"

"I don't want you to get hurt," she mumbled.

"So, you get hurt instead. What good is that?" She was furious, terrified she'd lose Charley.

Suddenly, there were people all over the room. The only one she recognized was the officer who took her to her cell and told her he didn't believed she had killed Ted. He asked which way Jalinsky went.

She pointed. "Don't kill him," she yelled and wondered why she'd said that. Maybe it was because of his wife.

Both Charley and Dave were put on gurneys. Charley was given fluids before they left the condo, and both were loaded into ambulances.

Evie called the first window company she found on her phone and told them it was an emergency. She hardly noticed Angie hanging around her.

"You go, Mom. I'll take care of the window and clean up the floor. I'll come over as soon as I can."

She gave Angie a kiss and hug and left, following the fading sounds of the sirens.

As she sat in the hospital waiting room while Charley was in surgery, she phoned Jalinsky's wife and gave her his message.

"I knew he was in some sort of trouble. Thank you for calling," she said with a sob. "I hope no one was hurt."

"Three were hurt, including your husband."

She went to Dave's room. Her son was lying very still, his face, even his lips, as white as the pillowcase. She pulled down the blanket and saw that his side was wrapped. A dot of blood marked the bandaging. His eyes opened.

"Mom, I've got a killer of a headache." He winced and his eyes closed. "How is Charley?"

"In surgery. Rebecca's on her way. When the window is fixed, Angie will be over."

The door opened and Rebecca came in. Evie told her about Charley and thanked her for coming.

She hurried through the halls to the surgery waiting area, where Charley's mother and father and her two brothers were seated. They stood as she entered. Reenie hugged her and introduced her husband, Charles. No one said anything as a doctor came out, wearing scrubs. He was the one who had talked to Evie earlier before she called Charley's family. He smiled and some of her tension melted away.

"She'll be all right. She lost a lot of blood. We replaced it. We took two bullets out, one from her arm and one from her thigh. Her neck was just grazed. She'll be staying here for a couple of days in case she needs more blood or fluids. Then she can go home. A nurse will come and dress her wounds. They're putting her in ICU right now. You can see her for ten-minute visits, one at a time. Don't get her riled up."

Evie stood next to Charley's bed and stared at her. She looked bloodless, pale against the pillow. Then she opened those gray-blue eyes and smiled.

Evie choked back tears and attempted to smile. "How do you feel?"

"Terrible. Did you get the window fixed?" Her voice sounded weak.

"Think so. Angie offered to take charge of that and cleaning up the floor. She'll be here as soon as it's done."

"Good girl." Her eyes began to close.

"Your family is here. We get to see you for ten minutes at a time."

"Can you stay when they're here?"

"Maybe. I'll ask."

A nurse came in. "Ten minutes are up." She was a young thing with kind eyes and a brown bob.

"I want her to stay when the others come in. I don't want her to leave," Charley said, head raised a little. Panting, she fell back on the pillow.

"I'll tell the head nurse," the girl said and left.

Reenie came through the door and Evie stepped back and sat down. "Hey, how's my girl?"

"Mom. I've been better. How are you?" Charley said.

"No one shot me up. Makes me think we should use regular bullets."

Charley's smile stretched into a grin, even her gums were white. She said, "I was thinking that too, but I don't think he meant to kill us. I think I jumped the gun." She smiled again.

Her mother did not. "Why was he there?"

"He was on the run. He might have taken one of us as hostage. Evie's two kids were there."

That had never occurred to Evie. She frowned, unwilling to think about it.

"Are you coming home when they release you?" Reenie was holding her daughter's hand.

"Thanks, Mom, but I'm going home with Evie. She'll be there if I need help."

Reenie turned to Evie. "When you need to go somewhere, give me a call. I'll come over."

"I will. Thanks," Evie said.

She went out in the hall when Charley's dad entered the room.

CHAPTER TWENTY-FIVE

Evie was watching a kingfisher swoop over the lake, and listening to the keening of cedar waxwings in a tree overhead, when Angie dropped into the empty chair beside her.

"Dave and I are leaving Sunday. Mom, I'm so glad I had this time to get to know Charley. She's gorgeous and smart and fun." She was looking at the lake, too. "I'm so relieved it all worked out. What if I'd lost you, Mom? I don't think I could stand that."

Evie smiled. "But you didn't. When do I meet this young man of yours?"

Angie met her eyes. "He's not the guy for me, Mom."

"I see. Well, when you do find that person, I want to meet him."

"I'll bring him home. I promise." Angie laughed. She no longer seemed uptight and critical. "Mom?"

Evie looked into her daughter's eyes again. Her skin was tan, her curly hair in a tight ponytail. "What, sweetie?"

"I was so proud of you after Charley was shot and Dave was knocked out. You just sort of took control."

"Really? You thought that?" She'd been terrified for Charley and Dave.

"Yeah. I did. He could have shot us all, but you told him if he killed Charley, he'd spend his life in prison."

She studied her daughter. "Thank you," she said, thinking it was all in how one perceived things. If her daughter wanted to think of her as some sort of heroine, when she'd been horrified and scared at the time, she guessed that was okay.

Her children were once again leaving, but they'd be back. They would never really leave her. She followed Angie upstairs where Dave and Charley were waiting on the deck in front of Evie's family cottage.

After Angie and Dave left on Sunday, it seemed quiet to Evie. She and Charley were sitting on the deck. Charley was working, and she was reading. She put her Kindle down when a pileated woodpecker called somewhere nearby. From across the lake, she heard the rusty call of sandhill cranes.

Evie felt Charley's eyes on her and met her gaze. "What?"

"It's lovely here," Charley said.

"It can't quite measure up to a bungalow on an island in the…" The look on Charley's face shut her up.

"Why do you have to make comparisons? Do you remember the shack in the swamp where I first took you? This place leaves that one in the dust. It's beautiful here."

"Thank you." She'd forgotten the shack in the wetlands that was burned down by someone who was after her. "I'm sorry. It's just that I'll never have the money you do, and it's not even that I want that kind of money. But I don't like being beholden, not even to you, whom I love."

"It's not my money that bought the island or the plane or the swamp, and I love you too."

"I know you do. That's another thing. You almost lost your life because of me."

"If I hadn't pointed a gun at Jalinsky, he might not have shot me. I've been thinking about that. You never believe you're going to die, until you almost do."

"That gun of yours invites death. Maybe the rubber bullets you use don't kill people, but the regular bullets everyone else uses do."

"Jalinsky is probably in Central or South America. They're watching his wife and will follow her if she goes anywhere."

"Much as I hate to leave, I think it's time to go home. Don't you?" They had been at the cottage for three weeks. Part of Charley's recovery.

"I'm going to sell the condo. Too many bad memories, like your house," Charley said. She was still limping and using a cane. She hadn't said it hurt to walk but Evie knew it did. "We'll buy a place together."

When Evie completed her course, she could take the test for her teacher's license. She wanted to teach the early grades, kids like the first graders she'd worked with. She knew, though, that she'd never make the money Charley did. When the differences between their incomes had come up, Charley had said they'd apportion the money. If Charley made one-third more than Evie, then Charley would pay one-third more than Evie.

"Can't we stay another day or two?" Charley's voice broke into her thoughts.

"I suppose." She would happily spend the rest of the summer here. She had thought Charley was probably getting antsy to get back to the office and was pleased to hear she wanted to stay longer.

"Is there any way I can get down to the water?"

"I could ferry you over from the landing in the boat, but you can't swim until the doctor says you can."

"Maybe next time we're here," Charley said.

Evie studied Charley, who had not yet regained the weight she lost after being wounded. She looked gaunt but happy. Next time, Evie thought, breathing in the smell of pines and feeling the whisper of a soft breeze. She would look forward to next time.

Bella Books, Inc.

Women. Books. Even Better Together.

P.O. Box 10543
Tallahassee, FL 32302

Phone: 800-729-4992
www.bellabooks.com